Falling for Nash

SOPHIA SUMMERS

KINGS ROW PRESS

READ ALL BOOKS BY SOPHIA SUMMERS

JOIN HERE for all new release announcements, giveaways and the insider scoop of books on sale.

Cowboy Inspired Series
Coming Home to Maverick
Resisting Dylan
Loving Decker
Falling for Nash

Her Billionaire Royals Series:
The Heir
The Crown
The Duke
The Duke's Brother
The Prince
The American
The Spy
The Princess

Read all the books in The Swoony Sports Romances
Hitching the Pitcher
Falling for Centerfield
Charming the Shortstop
Snatching the Catcher
Flirting with First
Kissing on Third

Vacation Billionaires
Holiday Romance

Her Billionaire Cowboys Series:
Her Billionaire Cowboy
Her Billionaire Protector
Her Billionaire in Hiding
Her Billionaire Christmas Secret
Her Billionaire to Remember

Her Love and Marriage Brides Series
The Bride's Secret
The Bride's Cowboy
The Bride's Billionaire

INTRODUCTION

Emery is trapped. Nash wants to save her. It would help if they got along.

The youngest Dawson brother is funny on the outside and tender on the inside. He has a drive to succeed and a passion for the rodeo. The family thinks he's outgrown them, but really, he has dreams of his own, and they're all about the Dawson Ranch. But first he has to either move on from Emery Banks or convince her to be the woman in his life.

A talented new barrel racer steps into the rodeo scene and takes the world by storm. And immediately gets under Nash's skin. She's too good, too opinionated. And too dang beautiful for him to simply ignore. And she's being pursued by the man who controls everything that side of town—the so called rodeo boss himself and one of Nash's biggest sponsors.

She's hard to win for any man, but she seems to appreciate the attention from the sponsor. Nothing is easy in this last-ditch effort to impress her before he retires from the rodeo scene altogether and returns home to the Dawson Ranch.

Read this not quite enemies to lovers romance, the last of the Dawson family ranch romances, and get hooked on a few more characters while you're at it.

CHAPTER 1

$\mathcal{N}$ash got off the phone with his brother, Mav. He rotated his shoulders a few times and then dropped to the ground to do push-ups. He loved his brother. But sometimes, the man rubbed him wrong. It wasn't his fault. He was the oldest and felt like their father. But Nash's dad had stopped meddling in his life when he was alive. There was no need to start up any kind of meddling now that he had passed.

Mav meant well, and the guy had been through enough in his life that Nash just took it. He powered through twenty more push-ups. He'd acquired some pretty large pecs because of this new method of dealing with Mav.

The family was getting together for Willow Creek Days, and they were wondering if Nash would be there. He had hedged, partly because he was making good money riding bulls, and he didn't want to miss out on prize money. But also because, while they didn't know it, he had his own hand in Willow Creek Days, and for some reason, he didn't want them made aware just yet.

But the good news was, they were hearing hints of a national rodeo showing its face in his town, and if that were the case, Nash could earn prize money and make his family happy all in the same weekend.

Once he'd finished about one hundred and fifty push-ups, he grabbed the keys to his truck. One twist of the key and it started right up. That, at least, was a good sign today would improve. His truck was old, beat-up, and semi-reliable. But he loved it. He could have asked Mav to trade it for one of the other trucks at the ranch. They used them all for promotional ad space. The logo and brand of Dawson Ranch was on every vehicle. But Nash didn't like asking for help, and he didn't like feeling like he was bleeding off the ranch money.

He pulled into the arena. His horse was there, as well as a group of practice bulls, and Nash needed to get up on both to clear his head and put in some practice times before the rodeo tomorrow night.

The sky was blue. It stretched large and wide across the Texas sky. One thing Texas did right was a bright blue sky. The polarized lenses on his sunglasses made the grass greener than usual as well. The fields around him seemed variated in color. His smile grew. Today was going to be a good day for sure.

"Nash!"

His good thoughts screeched to a halt.

"Isaiah." Nash tipped his hat and then waited for the man who ran his largest sponsor to catch up to him. "How you doing?"

"Doing just fine, just fine." He reached for Nash's hand and they shook.

"You here to see a practice time on Spitfire?"

Isaiah blinked, looking confused for a moment, and then

smiled. "Sure, man. I'd like to see that."

The man looked distracted. He searched the parking lot and shielded his eyes to check the entryway in front of them.

A car pulled up behind. Nash turned and his attention was immediately captured. Emery Banks hopped out of her old, beat-up Chevy truck and waved with a large, cheerful smile in their direction.

Nash's jaw about dropped to his boots. Never in all the time he'd known Emery did she smile at him like that.

He raised his hand, ready to welcome a new Emery, but she called out, "Isaiah, you ready to ride?"

Nash turned to the overly pleased man at his side and crossed his arms. "Really?"

Isaiah only gave him half a notice. "Really what, dude? Worry about your own performance."

"Hey, I've got nothing against a little flirtation with a client . . ." He did have a lot against it, particularly this client, but it wasn't his place to say. And Emery wasn't technically a client yet, which made the whole thing stink in Nash's opinion.

"You afraid she's gonna beat you out tonight?"

He scoffed. "No. Come on, Isaiah, I'm your biggest moneymaker around here, and not expecting to be unseated anytime soon."

"Unless we start putting some attention in on our Emery there. She's a gold mine."

Nash watched Isaiah's eyes follow Emery in a way that made him suspect she might be a potential gold mine in the man's mind in more ways than one. Nash bristled, but what could he do about any of this? A sponsor getting romantically involved with a potential client? A powerful man showing romantic interest in a woman who might benefit financially from the relationship? Both ideas didn't sit well, but what really chapped his hide? Emery deserved much better than that weasel Isaiah. She deserved a Dawson. Nash Dawson, to be precise. The problem being he just couldn't get along with her. She ignored him in all the most aggravating ways.

Like now. She approached Isaiah, all smiles and eyes for him. "You're here?"

"I told you I'd come, didn't I?"

"Yes, but I didn't know it would be so soon. I just rode last night, but I can go again."

"I'd like that. If I can get it on video, I can show the board. There's definitely more room on our team for another rodeo client—right, Dawson?"

He'd been trying to edge away. "I think that depends. Is there room? Some events bring in more money than others."

He wasn't trying to say anything, but Emery's eyes narrowed. "Too bad bull riding isn't as profitable as it was in its days of glory."

He rotated his neck to get rid of a sudden crick. "What are you trying to say? You implying that bull riding isn't making money?"

"I don't think I was implying. I think I just came out and said it. After you dropped that line about some events make more money than others—arrogant bull-riding nonsense—the obvious had to be said. Bull riding isn't the only money-maker anymore."

Isaiah whistled. "Now that, Dawson, was a proper shake-down." He grinned. "Come on, darling, show me what you got." He looked over his shoulder as they walked away. "I need to see you, too, Nash. Put on a good show for the board."

He lifted a hand to almost shoo the two of them away, but they weren't looking, nor did they care.

Nash frowned all the way to his horse. He didn't really need Lightning right now, but something about that Emery woman drove him to his horse every time. He got out a brush and ran it over Lightning's back. He'd be riding in with the opening parade on Saturday, and he wanted to run through the steps with him before then. Tonight would have been a good opportunity. Maybe it still would be. But it seemed more difficult with Isaiah in town and watching people. He draped his arm over the back of his horse. "You wanna ride tonight, big man?"

His horse nickered and pawed the ground.

"Hey now. I gotta ride the bulls too, you know. But I ain't cheating. You're the only animal for me."

"You sure about that, cowboy?" Dakota Henries leaned her arms over the fence, looking him up and down as if she wanted something, which he knew she didn't.

"Pretty sure." He tipped his hat. "How you doing, Dakota?"

"Oh, I'm doing what I always do." She tossed her extra-blond hair over her shoulder. "And I ain't too happy about it."

"What? Now, I know I need to catch up. What are you doing that you always do? You talking about helping your dad as the stock contractor? Or you talking about racing? And what aren't you happy about?"

"That's too many questions." She shook her head. "But I'll answer one of them. I'm not happy about the fact that I have to go up against your woman today with Isaiah watching."

He frowned. "You're not even cute when you're ridiculous. She's not likely to be my woman when Isaiah is making eyes at her." He frowned. "You looking for a sponsor?" Nash always took her for more of the family woman. She was a shoo-in to take over the business from her father—handling, breeding, providing the animals, not riding them.

"I wouldn't complain if I had a sponsor. I'd like to ride more."

"But you're complaining about riding today?"

"I can't go up against Emery. I'll never win a sponsorship that way."

He couldn't disagree. "But Isaiah isn't the only sponsor out there."

"The only one that matters."

He supposed that was true, especially for barrel racers. "I don't know what to tell you. Do your best?"

She swatted him with her gloves. "You're the worst kind of no help a barrel racer could ask for."

"My life's too complicated to worry about yours. I think you should stick to what you do best. Handle the stock. That's where the real money is." Didn't he know it. And that was exactly what he needed to talk to Maverick about. They needed to get that Dawson brand out as a stock manager. And Nash would be more than happy to get that going, as their manager. Mav could take care of the ranch, the land, the whole family as far as Nash was concerned, but the youngest brother wanted a piece of that Dawson brand, and he wanted it on his own stock contractor business.

He rotated his shoulders. Prize money. All he needed was more money and he would have a significant initial investment. His bones ached. His knees and hips might not function as they should ever again. But he was young. He had enough wins left in him. By his calculations, even if Mav didn't want to make an initial investment, Nash could still make it work.

Dakota was saying something Nash wasn't hearing. Then she huffed in his direction and stomped away toward her own stall, presumably to get ready to ride.

Dakota Henries wanted to ride. Nash smelled an opportunity there, possibly an in to some excellent stock from her family business. If Dakota wasn't interested in the animal side of things, Nash most certainly was.

Later that night at the rodeo, Nash adjusted his grip on the straps at the top of an angry bull. But the animal wasn't angry enough. If Nash wanted full points for this ride, the bull had to be downright furious. He had to want to ram a horn through Nash's gut.

Nash dug in a little bit with his heels, nothing to hurt the huge animal, just to irritate him. Spitfire kicked up his legs and hit the back of the very small chute. Excellent. "We have a live one." He grinned at the chute boss.

Tony clucked his tongue. "That you do. Now let's see if you can do something with this opportunity." He dipped his hat. They both turned out, waiting for that buzzer.

The arena was packed.

Spitfire shifted again beneath Nash.

Nash tugged at the ropes to make sure they were good and tight.

Everything in the whole arena went silent and moved slowly. Nash measured his breaths. The buzzer sounded. The gate opened. He raised one hand in the air, the other gripping and stubborn. Bull verses Nash, and Nash always won.

At least that's what he told himself, even when he got thrown off and nearly trampled. This was his pep talk. Nash —100, bull—0. And it wasn't going to be any different tonight. Prize money. It was all about the money.

The bull kicked up his back legs and then lifted his front

and turned a full clockwise circle with all four hoofs in the air. Nash had seen his ilk before, and he wasn't going to let some Spitfire ton hulk of a beast get the better of him.

Not a half breath later, Nash found himself lying in the dirt, forcing air into a tight and painful chest. The bull kicked up his legs. One of the fighters lugged Nash away. Every reaction in him was sluggish. He tried to thank the man, but noises, jibberish, came out of his mouth instead. "What the?"

"Stop talking, Nash. No need to let Isaiah get wind of a concussion." Tony, their best bullfighter, helped him to his feet while the others got the bull directed back to his pen, where water, hay, and food waited. Nash blinked. Did that bull look like he was prancing around? He had unseated Nash? He groaned. He'd just lost a crap ton of prize money. A piercing knife cute through his head.

Hours later on the medic's table, the man wasn't making any sense.

Finally, the doctor held a phone up to Nash's ear. "Nash, honey."

"Mom?" He glared at the man. Really? He called his mom?

"Yes, it's me. Now, he says you're not understanding him. You've got a concussion. A crack in your skull."

"I know what a concussion is. Mom, I'm fine. It's the first few hours after that we're concerned about."

"He doesn't want to clear you to ride, and since you're not making sense half the time, he called me. Thanks for putting me down as authorized to make decisions on your behalf."

"That's only if I'm incapacitated or mentally incapable." Those were the words he thought he'd said, but instead, half of them exited his lips, the other half a massive amount of unintelligible syllabic mess.

CHAPTER 2

*E*mery Banks watched from around the corner while the doctor signed some kind of paperwork, and Dakota helped Nash to his car.

"You're not gonna let him drive!" She gasped. No one could hear her, but the words had formed outside her thoughts anyway. They just came tumbling out of their own accord. But then her shoulders relaxed when Dakota put Nash firmly in the passenger seat.

"Good woman." She laughed at herself. "Come on, Emery. He drives you crazy. You're not his girl." She brushed her hands off on her jeans. "He's off your radar now, out from under your skin, so far from bothering you, you'd have to go find him to get a dose of the Nash heckling."

It was meant to be a cheerful pep talk, but instead all it did was descend her mood lower. She was gonna miss Nash Dawson. That was just how it worked with him. Like any itch or scab or . . . She sighed. Good piece of chocolate. The more attention you gave to whatever it was, the more it got to you, the more you itched at it or ate it. And she'd wanted to do both—itch at Nash and enjoy him. Her thoughts stayed with her all the way back to her trailer.

Curse her normal female reaction to a really good-looking man. What could she do if she responded to his broad shoulders, wide smile, and deep blue eyes like any woman would? He was hot, as hot as they came. And she was not immune. But with every second or third glance toward Nash, the more she wanted to lash out at his overly handsome face. She didn't need to be hooking up with any bull riders, none. And she didn't need to be pining after one either. She'd seen what happened to all the women who'd wanted to be at Nash's side. Not a single one was there.

If she'd just give it a try, she'd know once and for all, but she didn't want to give him the satisfaction of adding her to the list of women he'd rejected.

And she didn't want him, really. She knew what this was. Attraction only, plain and simple. And she knew what to do with that.

She took one more look in the mirror and then tried to get ready for a date with Isaiah. There was a man who could actually go places. He was as handsome as any other cowboy, almost. But not everyone could be as eye catching as Nash. Not every man melted her insides if he smiled. It was a good thing, where Emery was concerned, that his smiles were rare.

She couldn't control her tongue. And all that pent-up frustration, spurred on by denied attraction, brought out the most stubborn, blunt mouth she was capable of.

But now he was off to the hospital for head scans. And he'd lost the rodeo. And Isaiah had already mentioned to her how the sponsor wasn't going to be pleased with Nash. He'd said it like it was a good thing for Emery. But she didn't want to acquire a sponsorship at the cost of Nash's.

That made her the worst businesswoman ever, she supposed. And not very competitive. But she'd not win anything on the back and misfortune of another. It was not her way.

She sighed.

Which was probably why she still rode without a sponsor.

And which was why she needed to smile at Isaiah more. She cringed at her own behavior. But a little networking and friendly banter couldn't hurt things in that area. The sponsorship Isaiah could offer would do much more for her than anything else.

Her phone rang. She picked up without a second thought, even though she was mere minutes from being late and still needed to spice up her makeup. Her sister's calls were never without some sort of drama. "Lacey, what is it?"

The moan on the other end sent a panic through Emery that had every hair on her arms standing on end. "Where are you? Are you all right?"

"I'm fine. I mean, not really. Emmie." Her kid sister's voice shook, and the gasping breaths and shuddering sobs caused Emery's mind to race through all the possibilities. She broke up with her boyfriend last week. Could be related. Was she hurt? Fired from her job? Worse thoughts crowded in, but Emery pushed them out.

"I just need to come visit."

Emery almost groaned out loud. "Why? Talk to me, Lace, but talk fast because I have a date."

The wailing commenced. "Nooo! I'll never have another date again."

Emery relaxed a little bit. Her sister was lonely. She didn't have a man doting on her twenty-four seven because Kyle had turned out to be a loser and she broke up with him. And now she wanted a guy. Emery could handle that kind of drama.

"Oh, come on. You date more than a lead singer. What's the matter?" Emery applied her lipstick, hoping her sister would start talking.

"Kyle wanted back in."

Emery rolled her eyes.

"But of course I told him no way. But then all his best friends have been calling, trying to talk me into it. Except they're totally hot too, but now they won't go out with me. And that's like half of the whole social group." She sniffed. "Really and truly, I'll never date again."

"Why is coming here going to help with any of that? I don't have anyone to date."

"I thought a new group, change of pace . . ." Her voice drifted off. "Cowboys can be hot."

Emery could almost see the pout. She could definitely hear it. "No."

The gasp was almost amusing. "No? You won't let me come?"

Emery groaned. "Of course you can always come. But sis, you're not dating these cowboys. If you come, you can help me. Work." She smiled, knowing how hard that would go down.

"Okay." The sniffs grew quieter.

"Wait, what? You want to come here and help me work?"

"Sure. I got fired. I can't pay the rent. And I've got no one. I'm coming." She kissed into the phone. "Thank you, Ems. I love you so much!"

"Great! See you soon."

"Tomorrow!" More kisses and then the phone went dead.

And Emery wanted to sink to the floor. This could not be happening. The tightness in her chest wrapped strong cords around her, squeezing with intensity.

Every guy within ten miles was suddenly going to be standing at her trailer door. And she didn't want to deal with it.

She didn't want to deal with all the pampering, the beauty products, the clothes. She hung her head. "I don't have time or space for this."

But there was nothing she could do about it. She was all her sister had. Their parents were never really helpful anyway, but they were both gone. If Emery said no, Lacey really didn't have anywhere else to go.

The knock at her trailer door made her jump.

"Emery?" Isaiah surely heard her squeal.

"Yep! Just a second!"

"Can I come in? I brought something for you." He turned the handle and stepped in before she could answer. She closed the door to the bedroom, where she was taking a last-minute look in the mirror. She had nothing to hide, but she also wasn't ready to look at someone else just yet. She stared in the mirror. *You can do this. Lacey is your sister. She will grow up one day. Maybe today is the day.* She breathed deeply twice.

"You okay in there?" Isaiah sounded like he was approaching.

"Yep. Great." She opened her door, stepped out, and closed it behind her. No need to be seeing beds or thinking about beds on this date. "Ready?" She pointed behind him toward the kitchen and door to leave.

"Relax. Emery, sit down a minute. The movie doesn't start until nine."

She nodded slowly. "We're going to a movie?"

"I thought it would be fun, you know, the typical dinner and movie kind of date?"

"Yeah, that's great." She tried to sound into this. She really wanted to be interested. He was a good-looking man, certainly powerful. And obviously interested. What was wrong with her attraction buttons? She wanted to fiddle and nudge them, maybe give them a kick start. Here was a perfectly great, smart man. *We like smart men.*

But even when he held up a wrapped gift, she felt nothing for this man.

"What? You didn't have to bring me anything."

"I know. But you're worth it. I had fun picking it out. Open it." His smile was hopeful, and for a second, she was kind of endeared to him for even thinking of such a thing.

But the sponsor swag she pulled out of the wrapped box was less than thrilling, until he nudged her. "Lift it out."

Underneath was a small card. "Welcome to the Bunson sponsor team."

Her emotion choked up her throat. "Really? I'm in?"

He nodded. "We'll need to sign contracts and make it official, but I got the go ahead from the board to let you know. We are thrilled with your riding. You're the next up-and-comer for barrel racing and for all events. We want to push the women of rodeo, and you are going to become our poster client." His grin couldn't be larger, and the warmth that filled Emery overwhelmed even her sense for a moment, because she flung himself into his arms. "Thank you, Isaiah, this means everything to me. You have no idea how much I need this."

His arms softened around her and pulled her close, his hands moving, caressing. "Well, this is nice." Her gratitude hug was suddenly becoming much more intimate.

She stepped back. "Oh my gosh. I'm so sorry." She wasn't sure where to look or put her hands, but she knew they had to get out of her trailer right then. She stepped closer, swiveling to show that she was heading for the door. "Should we go?"

He put a hand out to pause her movement, resting a giant palm on her hip. "Hey, don't worry about that. We're friends at least. I'm taking you on a date. That's all separate from the sponsorship thing. I appreciated the hug." His eyebrow lifted, and he grinned at her in such a disarming way, she relaxed a little.

"Yeah, right. Okay. Sorry. Again. This is weird for me, trying to separate it all out."

"I'm as happy as you are the board wanted you. Of course, I gave them my glowing assessment of your market potential, but it was up to their decision. And my personal feelings aside, I feel the offer is well deserved, and generous." He nodded. "But now, if it's gonna be weird, let's put that here on your table, leave it, and just go enjoy dinner and a movie?"

Emery nodded. She could do that. Maybe. "Okay, great. And really, thank you."

"You're welcome." He put a hand at the small of her back. "Now, even though I'm liking you here all to myself, this is our first date after all." His wink brought a blush to her cheeks. She knew it. She couldn't control the cheeks.

And he noticed too.

But her blush was more from embarrassment and the idea of anyone thinking they'd shared this trailer for any other purpose.

She could have died at the thought.

As they stepped out onto the gravel, an all too familiar voice, all too close, laughed. "Well, would you look at that. Isaiah Hansen and Emery Banks getting a little cozy?"

She inwardly seethed. "Nash." She followed Isaiah out the door. "Are we twelve now?"

"Oh no, he's just feeling left out because he wasn't invited to the meeting."

Nash's eyes lit with interest.

"Business meeting, Nash. But now we're off for some pleasure. Some of us know how to separate the two."

Emery squinted her eyes at the blatant accusation sent in Nash's direction. One summer, he'd won first place, highest points across all judges. And it was later discovered that he was dating one of the judges' daughters. No big deal. But the papers had run with it as a scandal for a while. It hadn't affected his riding or his other scores, so it mostly blew over, but Isaiah was kind of a jerk to bring it up.

Nash didn't miss a beat at all. He thumbed his belt loops and rocked back and forth. "Emery and I have been able to handle it for years. You're the new piece to this puzzle." He smiled, but his eyes were serious and he held Isaiah's gaze for longer than Emery thought necessary.

Isaiah tipped his hat, then held open his car door. "And now you and I are going to have some real fun."

She slid in, glancing at Nash real quick. His eyes were full of caring, interest even. He tipped his hat and she smiled. What was that all about? They'd been doing it for years? Were they friends? Sure, frenemies. There was no one she knew better than Nash, except for Billy.

Then Isaiah shut her door and approached Nash.

If she could see through Isaiah's broad back, she might

have seen Nash's expression or had a hint of what they were talking about, but as it was, all she saw was Nash's stance shift from leaning back against a tree to stiff and balanced. Were they going to fight?

She put her hand on the door handle, but then Isaiah moved around to the driver's side. Nash's back was already turned and Isaiah hopped in the car.

"Everything all right?"

He rotated his neck for a moment. "With Nash? Sure. You know him. Regular bread and butter client of Bunson. He's doing great." Isaiah adjusted the rearview mirror. When he turned back to Emery, his easy smile had returned and he seemed to be the same Isaiah she was getting to know.

CHAPTER 3

ash was pretty sure he had just witnessed Emery signing on as a client of Bunson. A part of him was thrilled for her. He knew she was looking for something, and Bunson was the most lucrative, the best way to get her name out there. But a part of him filled with the dead weight of a bunch of broken-down tractor equipment. She was in a tough spot, trying to keep Isaiah happy to save her career.

It didn't sit well. It just didn't. He wasn't any happier about it seeing it unfold right before his eyes than he had been thinking it was coming. It was a low move, even for Isaiah, and someone had to stop that man. Someone who didn't also rely on him for a good amount of his income.

His head hurt, like he'd cracked his skull or something. The doctor said it was real mild, but it wasn't his first. He'd never been told that before, but he knew he'd had at least another. The MRI had shown him two others. And that was about as many as a fellow was allowed to get in his life before he needed to turn over the reins to a man who still needed a little brain damage.

Nash watched Isaiah's car drive out of sight, the dust swirling and floating in the air long after it was gone.

He plopped down in one of his lawn chairs and then regretted the jarring motion as a slice of pain reminded him that he still had a brain. With one hand cradling his head and the other reaching for his Tylenol, he considered his options.

The doc said he had two. Keep riding and die. Or stop and live. But Nash knew that was what all docs would say, and he was grateful they said things like that. Every man needed an ultimatum now and then. But what Nash knew was that he still had a few good rides in him, and that would be enough to round out his prize savings with an extra zero on the end of the number. And that might be enough to buy out a small stock contractor.

But not enough to get the children's center to where it needed to be in Willow Creek. That would come. He could start building it up with the extra money from the stock earnings.

He closed his eyes. If he could just finish a complete season, he'd be where he needed to be as long as he kept winning. He'd have enough for the children's center and stock contractor buyout.

He winced. The idea of getting back up on a bull with such a tender head was too much even for him. The doctor had demanded a solid four weeks anyway.

Long into the night, he opened his eyes, still sitting in his chair outside the trailer door. He must have fallen asleep. A soft voice approached with the steps from nearby. "You waiting up for me, cowboy?"

His neck felt like it had a new permanent limit on motion. He held it behind his head while slowly tipping it from side to side and then forward and back. "Not exactly. What time is it?"

"It's ten thirty." Emery sat down in the chair beside him.

"That's kind of early. Bad date?"

She sighed. "No. It was great. He was a gentleman. And he suggested that we both have an early morning tomorrow so we should call it a night." She shrugged.

He held his head so he could look at her without too much pain. Maybe that meant things didn't go very well. He could only hope.

"How's your head?"

"Right now, it's my neck that's rebelling. It won't hold my head up properly."

"You trying to sleep out here?"

"Fell asleep." He turned to her. "So, it was an all right date? He's . . . a good guy?" As soon as the words were out of his mouth, he wished to take them back. What was he doing? Trying to be her father here?

But she leaned back and nodded. "I think so. You know? I never thought I'd be in this place. But he offered me a spot. They want to sponsor me." Her smile grew. "And that's awesome. I need it."

He held up his fist for her to bump. "Welcome to the team. I'm happy for you."

"Thank you. It's gonna get pretty crazy for me." She turned to him suddenly, looking at him full in the face. It was dark, and the moon above put her eyes in shadow, but he could tell something intense was going on with her. All he could do was wait and sort of hold his breath, and his head.

"My sister Lacey is coming to stay with me."

Nash waited. But when she didn't say more, he asked,

"Isn't that a good thing? I've seen Lacey before, she's cool, fun." He chuckled. "The guys are gonna be real happy . . ."

But when Emery stiffened, he saw it might be a bit of the problem. "I mean, they'll stay away if we let it be known . . ." He was saying nothing right. Who knew why she had sat right there next to him. He had a chance to be something here, and his tongue wouldn't play nice with his brain.

Emery rubbed her head. "I don't know. She can take care of herself . . ." She winced. "Or she can't. I gotta look out for her, you know? And if she's far away, I can sort of ignore her choices, but if she's right here, I'm gonna feel like I have to manage things. She's a handful. A sweet, lovable handful." Emery sighed and lifted her chin to see the stars. "It sure is pretty out here when the lights are all off."

Nash wanted to reach for her hand. He wanted to place his on her back and rub it for a minute. Emery looked like a bundle of strung-up nerves. No wonder she seemed tense. Maybe it wasn't all about him. Maybe she was worried about a few too many things. "Can I help? Look out for her a little bit?" He had no idea what he was offering here. And it might come back to haunt him.

But her mouth curled up in a slow smile. "If I liked you more, I'd tell you to stay far away, but seeing as how you're an itch that just keeps on growing as far as I'm concerned, I might just take you up on that."

He laughed. "An itch? That's what I am?" He shook his head and then regretted it. "I think I can do better than an itch. How about a tickle?" He reached for her hand this time, bringing it up to his lips like a fancy gentleman. He couldn't believe it, but she let him. "I could be a friendly tickle."

"Like you're poking me in the ribs? Like you're twelve?"

she teased, but her eyes widened when his lips brushed the skin on her knuckles.

"Not a poke. I'm not twelve. Something just a little bit fun and a little bit . . . enticing."

She pulled her hand back. "That's not as bad as an itch."

He shook his head, slowly. "And I'll watch out for Lacey when I'm around. I have to chase the prize money. It's getting real."

"Can you ride?"

He didn't want to talk about his medical issues with her. Or with anyone. No one could know. The doc said he'd keep it quiet if Nash just did the four weeks' rest. "I'll be back up for Nashville. And an event back home."

"And in the meantime?"

He held his hands out. "At your service. Sister-sitter."

She laughed, sounding more carefree than she had in a while. "That might be your most regretted last words, but thank you." She rested a hand on his bicep for a minute. "Thanks a whole bunch. She's in a tough spot."

"I get it. Family is everything." He thought about mama. She was going to spit fire if she found out he was planning to keep riding as soon as one month from then. But if he told her, he would be marching himself back home to Dawson Ranch to be coddled and talked over. He'd tell her when it was all over. But then a memory surfaced. Had he talked to his mama from the medic's chair?

Emery sat beside him, looking up into the stars for a surprisingly long time. At first they were quiet. His neck relaxed. He closed his eyes. And then he asked, "What's your favorite constellation?"

She hummed to herself a minute. "The one with the three stars. What one is that?"

"Orion?" His voice was soft. "Mine too."

"What's your favorite country song?"

"Ballad or dance?"

"Both."

"Ballad—I like the ones that tell a story. Someone's always eloping with someone else, or the grandma is dying or something, but they're pretty and I like to feel good."

"Or bawl your eyes out." She laughed. "Okay, what about dance?"

"I love a good swing. Give me that beat, mmm, and I can dance any man off that stage."

"Oh, I'd love to see this."

"Would you?" He lifted his head. "Cause I'm not afraid of putting my money where my mouth is. You free tomorrow night?"

"You sure you can go dancing? You haven't moved your head much."

"I told you, that's a neck problem. And yes, I can go dancing." He thought so anyway. He wasn't missing this chance if he had to fill himself with pain meds to do it. "You in? Or are you afraid Isaiah might stop by and see you?"

Emery bristled right there in her seat like he hoped she would. "He doesn't own me."

"Oh yeah? Prove it."

She lifted a hand in the air. "I will. You're on."

"Eight o'clock, seven if you want dinner . . ." He let it dangle. It would make their fun dance challenge more like a date. Would she take it?

The pause was at least interesting. She considered him. "I think I'll get Lacey situated, and it'll be dancing only this time."

"This time?" Nash's smile grew. "Am I seeing an opening for other times?"

She fidgeted and then sat forward like she was going to get up. Dang it. He'd pushed too far. "I should probably call it a night."

"Right. Okay." He stood and winced.

"And Nash?"

"Hmm?" His head pounded as the blood tried to readjust itself somewhere inside.

"Thanks for helping out with Lacey."

"Anytime. We have to stick together. Family is family."

She looked like she might say more, but she rocked back and forth from heel to toe for a second and then turned and walked away. "Bye now." Her hand waved back over her shoulder.

CHAPTER 4

*E*mery kept walking even though her whole body was about to turn back around and stay as close to Nash as possible. She hummed with that yearning. His lips on her knuckles. His mouth, his hands—strong, rough, gentle. They'd had a normal conversation. No one digging into the other, not really. And he'd offered to help with Lacey.

Was this the same Nash she spit fire at more often than not? The same guy who walked around like bull riding was the only reason to have a rodeo? Oh, she was in trouble. If the Nash she hoped was underneath all that cocky swagger was as good as currently advertised, she would fall hard and deep whether she wanted to or not.

And from what she could tell, Nash didn't do girlfriends. He was as single as anyone in the business.

So basically, he was someone to stay away from.

And that was why she turned right around. "Nash?"

He stopped halfway up the steps into his trailer. He turned slowly, rubbing his neck.

"Watch yourself. Isaiah said you're on your way out if you're not careful."

He stiffened. "And why would he say that? To you?"

She stepped back at his tone. "Hey, you're helping me out with Lacey and I'm just trying to return the favor. I thought you'd want the inside scoop."

"From you? So you date the boss and I get the cast-off insults you hear while making dreamy eyes over dinner?"

Her fury rose inside like the lava screaming to the surface in a volcanic explosion. "Well, not anymore. Not if you're gonna get all bull rider on me. It was not an insult. It was a warning. I guess. I don't know." She was about to turn around, but instead she stepped closer. "I thought for one minute you were different, but really, you're just like all the others. You think this whole rodeo would shut down if you walked away."

He started to shake his head and then winced again. "I don't know what just happened here, but maybe we can rewind to the time we were talking nicely to each other. I have a headache and I'm going to bed." He opened his door, stepped in, and closed it behind him.

And now Emery remembered why she and Nash never got along. Because he was the most pompous, conceited, hard to talk to man she'd ever met.

She spun around and huffed it all the way to the next trailer, which was hers.

Why, oh why, had she parked next to him?

When she plopped down on her chair just inside, she realized she hadn't. He'd chosen the spot after she arrived.

Something softened inside. But only a little bit. He was probably just watching to see what she would be doing with Isaiah. Tugging off her boots and peeling off all the riding clothes, she knew she was being unfair. He was helping with Lacey, after all. He'd been a decent guy. He was hurting right now. It didn't matter.

She tried to brush him off, tried to wash thoughts of him away while she showered. But it was hard going. Nash was not easily dismissed from one's mind. Nor his touch from her hand. Even shower water could not ease the urge to have his lips return to her skin, anywhere. Knuckles would be fine. His mouth was soft—firm, but soft. And that was just what she imagined he would be. Strong, caring, soft on the inside. Stop. She told herself to stop. Nash Dawson was a good guy. Everyone knew it. But that didn't mean he was good for her. They couldn't talk for more than thirty minutes without going at each other about something. Tonight just proved it.

Emery threw a towel around herself. And now she'd agreed to dancing. Tomorrow. Well, dancing did not mean she was going to get starry eyed and let him have any kind of satisfaction regarding her interest. She could only be pleased she'd told him no dinner. Staring across the table at Nash over dinner was too much for her right now. She'd either explode in his face about something or turn dreamy. Neither could happen.

She spent the rest of the evening cleaning up her trailer and making space for Lacey. The woman came packed with more stuff than anyone who lived in a trailer should. They could bed at opposite ends. But that meant stretching it out on the other side. It was a feature Emery rarely used, but the whole back end could extend another four feet to create an additional bedroom. It took two people to make the extension. She'd pull out the crank and ask someone, not Nash, to help get that set up.

The water turned off in his trailer.

Perfect. They were both finished showering. This was gonna be a long stay in Mesquite, Texas. She had a rodeo every week for six. And a big national spot or two squeezed in. *Heaven help me.* She turned on some music. It was slow and nice, a local Christian station.

Heaven help me. She said that a lot, and thought it all the time. Usually in too casual a manner, if she were really trying to analyze things. Truth was, she desperately needed the help. Her flippant thought reminded her of a new challenge she was following. Someone, somewhere, had posted a daily reading devotional. And she wanted to follow along. She scrolled through her notes and then clicked on the site. This was too good. She looked up through the ceiling toward heaven. "Oh, you have a sense of humor, don't you?" The quote for the day and the reading challenge fell in Psalms 122:1-2. *"I lift up my eyes to the mountains—where does my help come from? My help comes from the Lord, the Maker of heaven and earth."*

Emery laughed to herself. "Heaven help me. Hah." But wasn't it so true? Tears stung her eyes. She let them fall. Letting God help. Grace. She knew about it all in theory. And she'd certainly seen the miracles in her life. Wasn't the fact that she and Lacey were both still standing a miracle all by itself? When left on their own, the two girls—and then women—just did the best they could. But that took some grit. And sometimes grit ignored help. You just had to cowgirl up and get the work done, or you wouldn't last.

But here, she saw how she could be soft. *"Where does my help come from? My help comes from the Lord, the Maker of heaven and earth."* She could let God in more. And maybe even recognize His hand when He helped. Surely He did. Her conversation with Nash outside came back to her. Nash had so readily agreed to help keep an eye on Lacey. Was he someone God had put in her life? She shook her head. *Nah.* She couldn't be thinking like that. But he was a nice enough guy to agree to help.

But then her mind started going through the memories. She usually blocked them out. It wasn't helpful to a person's confidence to remember all the hard moments with her parents, all the neglect, the times she and Lacey hid under her bed, hoping every adult in the house would forget they were there. And then her parents were sent to prison, and she and her kid sister went on the run, desperately trying to stay together until Emery turned eighteen. She smiled. They'd done it. But it had won them a life together with a fiercely independent nature.

Until she'd stumbled on the rodeo. Billy had found her sleeping in the hay, with her sister curled up beside her.

Emery shook her head. *You know, a woman learns to be real independent with the kind of life I've had.* Did she blame God? Not really. He didn't make her parents act like they did. And maybe God led her to rodeo and that had saved her. So maybe He was the good guy in the story. Of course He was.

She pulled out a pen and began scratching down some thoughts. That was the other part of the challenge, write what you thought about the verse. She laughed at her first sentence. *"The way I see it, God is in the details. But sometimes, He doesn't do much about it."* She kept writing. *"But . . . He's also there so integrally and connected that we don't see Him anymore. And that's sad. Try to see God more in your day and turn to Him now and then."* She underlined *"see God."* She studied her words for a moment and then nodded. Good enough. She was definitely not going to create one of those pretty bullet journals people were talking about making, with all the sticky notes and the cross referencing and everything. But it would be important and personal. And she had a good feeling about this new challenge.

She got down on her knees at her bed. "Thank you, God, for this challenge. I hope to learn more about You and to see Your hand helping me. I know You do. We probably wouldn't even be here if it weren't for Your help. Help me to see You more." Another tear fell. "Thank you."

A great warmth filled her small trailer. Something she had not created or brought into the room. She placed a hand at her heart in wonder. "Is this You?" The feeling only grew stronger. And she climbed into bed, hoping not to scare it away by too many thoughts or movement. Laughing to herself, she hugged her thoughts close. If God heard her, if He paid attention to her studies and her little journal, then He cared about her life. She was happy she'd said thank you. "Help me know what to do about Isaiah." Nothing came to mind. But she held onto the peace and comfort that her prayers and Bible study had brought. Things would work out. "Oh, and please help me not to lose it with Lacey." She laughed. That was one prayer she might need to repeat a few times.

The next day, Emery hurried out as early as possible, only to find Nash stepping out his door at the same time. She tried to paste a normal expression on her face, but he laughed. "Happy to see me?" His eyebrow rose up high, mocking her.

She could only shake her head. "We're a mess. I won't even be apologizing for losing it with you because I'm gonna do it again. You drive me a little bit crazy."

"Good crazy or bad crazy?" He smiled, warm, inviting.

When she had no immediate response, just burning cheeks and an opened mouth, he laughed some more. "Come on, Firestorm. It's time to get this rodeo going."

"You're helping out?"

"Sure, got nothing better to do. When does Lacey get in?" He checked his watch.

"This afternoon, I think. How's your head?"

"Feeling good, and my neck took a long, relaxing sleep while I thought over all the ways I'm arrogant and uncaring."

He gave her a decent sarcastic side-eye that she had to respect. Then she sighed. "Do you want me to spell it out?"

He held up his hands. "No. I've had enough honest tongue lashings to get me through a long day in the hot sun." He lifted up some wire cutters.

"No, you're mending fences?" She reviewed her opinion of him yet again. "That's some serious commitment, or you're a glutton. I can't tell what you have going on, but something is not sitting right. Oooh, you hit your head." She laughed until she snorted and then covered her mouth. "I'm sorry, but it's just so . . ."

"Easy? Yeah, pick on the guy with a brain injury. Real classy." He jumped onto a four-wheeler. "I'll see you on the other side of this day. Enjoy riding. You know, the thing I used to be able to do."

"Oh, stop your whining, Dawson. I'll tell your mama." Mr. Billy Thornton rested a hand on his shoulder. "Before you go out there sweating in all this heat, I wanted to catch a word."

"Yes, sir." Nash had all kinds of respect for the man who owned the Mesquite Rodeo. He was good and worked hard. His family had been around about as long as the Dawson name. And besides, his father had counted him as a friend. That was enough for Nash.

"What can I do for you, sir?"

"You mean, besides mending my back pasture fencing?" His eyes twinkled with respect.

"I'm off the bulls for four weeks."

"I heard."

"You did?" Just how much had he heard and from who?

"Yep. Dr. Terrance and I play golf. He mentioned a few things, off the record."

"He's not supposed to be doing that."

"True. And I'm not supposed to be talking to you right now. But we're all gonna suppose we don't know what the other is talking about. The thing we do know is that you're like family, Nash. And there ain't a rodeo in the world worth winning if you damage your brain. Every good man knows when to step away."

"I appreciate the confidence in me, sir."

Billy held his breath a moment, as if he might say something more, but he stopped, exhaled, and then gripped Nash's shoulder again. "You take care of yourself. If there's anything I can do, you let me know."

"I will, sir, and thank you." He softened toward the man, who had already done so much for him. "I'm working on something. I'm almost there, and I can step away after a few more wins."

He nodded. "I wish you the best of luck. And thanks ahead of time for all the work I know you're gonna be doing around here the next four weeks. A Dawson with nothing to do just doesn't exist in this world." He stepped back, chuckling to himself. "Take care."

"Thank you, sir."

Nash turned on the ATV, and then pulled around to the house. He'd be picking up a few more hands for this job.

CHAPTER 5

*M*ama Dawson sat still more often these days. She enjoyed a long swing on her back porch, a good book on her front couch. She had even taken up crochet. And of course, she loved her Bible. That soft, worn book with the marked-up and well-used pages had gotten her through decades of living. The quiet life suited her.

But not today. The kitchen pantry was about near driving her to an early grave, and if she didn't tackle it now, it was going to be one big chaos trying to get the meal on the table Sunday when all the kids came for dinner. As she took things off shelves and wiped them down, she admitted that keeping busy was helping her in more ways than one. She moved slower today. It was the anniversary of her dear Tommy's death. The hour was early yet, but none of the children seemed to be paying much attention to the day. Heaven knew they'd never forget their father, but the specific date? Who even knew if they were looking at their calendars.

Was that for the best? Would Tommy want them to mourn every year on a particular day? Or celebrate? More like he'd want them to get to work. Which was why she'd decided to gut out the pantry at five in the morning. Partly. There were other reasons.

Sleep didn't come or linger as long as it used to. She didn't have too much rushing through her thoughts nowadays. She did worry herself over Nash now and then. That boy needed to settle. But something told her he had things under control, and so she trusted that gut feeling and her boy. She could always worry about Grace. She was a beautiful teenager. But the girl also seemed to have things under control. And she was darling to check in on Mama almost every day. Decker and Faith and Dylan and Kate were doing well too.

The town had settled down in the mad rush to sell their properties. The new shopping and entertainment had been a boon for the town instead of an eyesore. The Dawson brand was learning to find income in diversified places. No, there wasn't anything to keep her up at night with worry. Her body just wanted to linger in the almost-sleep feelings for a time before drifting off, she supposed. And then the tiniest hint of light coming through the window was enough for her to get moving.

She took all her different containers out, one at a time, wiping them down with just a hint of vinegar. She believed in storing just a little bit extra. They could rotate through the non-perishables and have enough for a good ninety days if she was real careful about it. In today's world, you just never knew when the electricity, gas, or the supply chain would let you down in one way or another. Heck, they'd had enough runs on stores in the last few years for Mama to know she couldn't rely on others to always have what she needed.

Mav and Bailey had stopped by the other day. Grace was

going to be living with Mama that summer. Bailey had finally decided to do another tour. She'd written a couple songs, and they were so well loved around town, she'd pitched them to the producers, who scooped them up like the newest flavor of ice cream at Judy's. Mama was happy for them.

And what was super special about Grace was that she had a bitty hold on Nash's heart. The two of them had been planning the Center for Children in Willow Creek. No one else really knew or paid attention. But this was one of the better ideas to come out of the Dawson family. Mama knew Tommy would be proud. And she was looking forward to watching it all unfold. From the day Grace named her bitty pig Nash, she knew the two of them would be up to something someday. And this was perhaps that day. She could see Grace being invested in its creation and follow through over the years, and Mama admitted she loved anything that brought her boys closer to home.

But Nash was busy doing important things. For some reason, he was on her mind that morning. And as she hummed tunes from their Sunday hymn practice, she considered why that would be.

He was earning every last dollar in prize money. He hadn't confided in her his specific plan, but she suspected she knew. She'd been watching him choose rodeo after rodeo, taking top dollar. He had strategically managed his schedule with the most earning potential. What was he saving for? Heaven knew he wasn't spending any of it, not with his threadbare jeans and older than the hills hat. His truck practically broke down every time he touched it.

Her phone rang. Her smile grew to see Billy Thornton's name show up in her notifications. "Hey there, Billy."

"Milly. How good to hear your voice. If only I were eating your biscuits at the same time."

"Come on over."

"No man could turn down an invitation like that. I have to be in town first. And that's exactly why I'm calling."

"Oh? I thought you were going to let me check up on my son without his knowing."

He was quiet a moment too long.

"Billy?"

"No, no. I'm just laughing over here. Your Nash is the best we got. And he's a good man. Right now, he's out there mending my barbed wire."

"Why's he mending fence?"

"I just told you. I'm going to tell Mav next time I see him that Nash is the most helpful Dawson. He's already told me I've got the next four weeks to benefit from his generosity."

"Four weeks, huh?" Mama pressed her lips together. His head injury must have been worse than he let on.

"Now don't you go jumping to a mother's conclusions. I'm sure there's nothing going on other than a good rodeo man wanting to give back to his community."

"While I'm sure that is a lovely sentiment and he does give back, I'm gonna have to give my boy a call tonight to hear from his own mouth. Thank you for letting me know."

"Now, you didn't hear a thing from me. You know that."

"I'll keep your name out of it. I have my ways, Billy Thornton. You should know that."

"Oh, I know it, don't I?" He shuffled around on his end like he was messing with the things on his desk.

Mama waited.

"I'm calling about something." He paused. "There's really no better way to say this than to just spit it out. We have a woman here who's kind of like a daughter to me at this point. She's been with us since the day I found her trying to sleep in the barn. She's fun, capable, loves the work, and just got herself a new sponsor."

"Who?" At times, Dawson Ranch had been known to sponsor someone outside their family. But for now, Nash was the only one wearing the name, right next to the Bunson brand. She had to hand it to her family. They'd certainly made a name for themselves.

"Her name is Emery Banks. And she's good, real good. I even see her taking on Nash a bit—you know how the young folks go back and forth."

She smiled. "Yeah, I do." She and Tommy used to be much like that. They were not a love at first sight kind of couple, not really—though secretly, maybe a little bit. A girl would be plain stupid not to notice Tommy Dawson. And she certainly had. This Emery had just become someone of great interest to Mama. She had seen her ride. "I've met her. Such a nice woman, and tough as nails."

Was she sparring with Nash? Every bull rider needed to be taken down a peg or two. Everyone except maybe her Maverick. He'd been taken down way too many pegs. But they loved Bailey with all their hearts and the two belonged together. God worked His ways. That was one thing Mama had learned over the years. Listen up, do your part, and then get out of the way to see the Lord reveal His arm in all the ways He did best.

And while she much preferred all her chicks under her wings, she had also learned a thing or two about letting them peck around in the yard and fly.

"So what do you want me to do, Billy?"

"I'm looking at doing another rodeo in Willow Creek."

"That's a great idea! You won't believe all the buildup that's been going on. You'd have crowds for days."

"But would I have riders? Do we still have the people there to back it up?"

"Oh, for sure. We're just gearing up for our Willow Creek Days, and you should see the local talent that's showing up. Some of the young folks too, getting their first shot. Something worth considering. Can I ask why?"

"Just a hunch. I'm thinking it would be good for business." He sounded a bit more mysterious. And Mama didn't know what to think, but she wasn't going to be complaining about some more business in her town, nor about the chance to get Nash here local. "You're gonna attract the national talent as well."

"I hope so. We're gonna start traveling maybe. And the first stop is Mesquite Rodeo meets Willow Creek."

"That has a nice ring, doesn't it?"

"It sure does. Can I count on some of them biscuits if I plan a whole rodeo in your town?"

"You sure can. That and a heaping slice of my peach pie."

"Then I'm in—lock, stock, and barrel, as they say. I'll be seeing your lovely face in June, I reckon, which is also a perk in my mind."

Mama laughed, and her cheeks burned just a touch. "Oh you. You'll be seeing my face, that's for sure. Whether or not it's lovely after all these years is just a beholder kind of understanding." She made to swat him away, though he couldn't see her from the phone.

"I'll be the judge of that, Milly. And thank you. Maybe we could get some help talking it up too, when I got the details fixed just right."

"You can count on Dawson Ranch. Give us a sponsorship slot, will you?"

"Done. Signage everywhere. And maybe you have some stock we could borrow."

"Good trade if I've ever heard one."

"You're a good woman to do business with, you know? Remind me a lot of your son Nash."

"Oh? Is he taking after his mama? That's good to hear."

"I thought you'd think so. I'll be seeing you, Milly Dawson."

As soon as he hung up, she dialed her son.

His groggy voice answered, and she realized she and Billy had been having a friendly conversation at six in the morning. She shook her head. That was just how it went when you were old. Billy's wife passed away about the same time as Tommy. Maybe he just needed someone to talk to. They both did at this hour.

"Nash, honey?"

"Everyone all right?"

"Yes, don't you worry about a thing over here. I just forgot that the rest of the world isn't awake yet."

"Oh, mmm." Sounds of him moving around on his bed made her smile.

"You go back to sleep, son. I'll call you in a few hours."

"No, this is good. I'm about to get up anyway. Working with the stock this morning."

"Oh? You got some extra time on your hands?"

The pause was long, but Mama knew he would fill it.

"Yeah, Mom, Doc took me off riding for three and a half more weeks. So I'm just helping out."

"What was the diagnosis?"

"I banged my head, but don't worry. He said it's as hard as ever."

"Happy to hear that. Can't have your head getting soft." She laughed. "Was it a concussion?"

"Yeah."

She winced. "Son, you be careful. You're gonna want a really smart head on your shoulders when you get to be my age."

"I got a lot of years to be worrying myself over that, don't I?"

"Not as many as you think. Hey, Billy called just now."

"Oh?" The hesitation in Nash's voice was all she needed to know about the state of her son's health. He wasn't doing well, and he wasn't talking.

"Yep. And he said he's planning a rodeo out here in June. And I think he's coming out for Willow Creek Days to check it all out."

"A Billy Thornton rodeo in Willow Creek?"

"Yep. Thought you'd like to know."

"That's great. We need to talk to Grace, let her know."

"I knew you'd be thinking along those lines. Get those kids working the rodeo, getting one right here in Willow Creek again—that's a real good thing, isn't it?"

"It is, Mama. I have plans. And this is feeding right into them. If we can get a rodeo to stick, even better."

"I'd hoped so. Now, can you do me a favor and get me the phone number of that pretty little thing and her sister? What's her name?" She paused just for the fun of it. "Emery, right? Can you get me her number?"

"Ma, why are you wanting to call Emery?"

"Oh, just doing a favor for Billy. Now don't get all suspicious just because you have feelings for the woman."

"Ma, I don't . . . all right, I have a few feelings, but most of the time they aren't pleasant. We aren't gonna be a thing. So if this is motivated in some way to try to find me a wife—"

"Son, son, I'm not trying to find you a wife. I'm doing a friend a favor, that's it. And I love those girls. If you knew their story, you would love them too."

"I know their story."

"Probably not the whole thing, son. You give them lots of leeway."

His sigh was long, and it made her smile. "Lacey is showing up today, and I'm tasked with sister-sitting. Does that make you feel any better?"

"Oh yes. What a good son. I knew you wouldn't leave those ladies out to dry."

"Believe me, Mama, no one, not a single person, is worried about Emery Banks. She's got things all worked out. And she's tough as nails."

"Well, that's why I'm worrying about her, me and Billy, cause she's got the rest of the world fooled. Now off with you. Get to work now that you're awake. The sun's up and the Dawsons are up."

He chuckled. "I say that to myself every morning."

"Your father was a good man."

"He sure was. Thinking about him today."

"Thank you, son."

"And Billy. He's a good man too."

She gasped. "Nash Dawson. I don't know what you're trying to say right now—"

"I'm not saying a single blessed thing. But you just said a whole heck of a lot with your response." His laugh filled her ear. And she knew her face was warm, but nothing more was going to be said about Billy. "Goodbye, son."

"Bye, Mama, and don't worry, your secret is safe with me as long as Emery is safe with you."

"You know she is."

"That depends on our separate definitions of the word safe. But I gotta run, you're right. The sun might get hot before I'm even out in it."

"Can't have that. Love you, baby."

"You too. And Mama, I'm sorry about Dad. Today is gonna be a tender one."

Tears sprang to her eyes immediately, and she almost couldn't speak. "Thank you, son. He'd have been real proud of you."

"And he loved you more than all of it. He did it for you."

She nodded. "For all of us. Bye now."

Nash would always be her baby. He'd stopped trying to wiggle away from the title years ago. And she loved him fiercely, as fiercely as she did the others. But he wasn't right in the world yet. He'd not found his path. And of course, she'd love to see him married.

But either way, she'd have to find a way to keep him off a bull until his head was healed.

CHAPTER 6

*E*mery waited at the airport for Lacey to come out of baggage claim. She'd brought the cover for the truck so they could use the back bed to fit all of Lacey's bags. But when her sister stepped out of the automatic doors with one bag, Emery laughed in relief. She waved. "Sister!"

Lacey looked up from her phone. "Oh good!" She turned to look behind her. "She brought a truck. We're good."

And then a man exited with two luggage pull carts full of bags.

Emery pulled her sister into her arms. Her hair was newly highlighted, her nails perfect. She smelled like a salon and dressed like she was about to go on a cruise. "Sister." She squeezed her tight. "I've missed you." She looked into her face. "You seem well. So happy you're here." She looked at the tall, good-looking man who pushed the luggage cart. "With what looks like your whole apartment."

"Well, they're kicking me out. What was I supposed to do with it all?" Lacey pouted. "Also, this is Jerome. He was on the flight with me and so kindly stopped on his way out to help me with all this." She waved over it, and then flashed her lashes at Jerome, who stood taller.

"Thank you, Jerome. The truck is right here," Emery said.

They all unloaded the bags, which took up less room than Emery thought, and then she climbed into the truck while Lacey worked out whether or not to give this guy her number.

As soon as Lacey climbed in the truck, the smell of her fruity shampoo filled the air. Emery smiled. "It's good to see you."

"You too! Now, you're gonna have to put me to work! What's happening this weekend?"

"We have a rodeo tonight. And then another this weekend. And great news! I got a sponsorship!"

Lacey squealed. "That's so amazing! Who is it?"

"Bunson."

Lacey wrinkled her nose.

"Oh, come on, they're the best."

"I know. And it's all about the money, but does that mean we have to hang out with that guy? What's his name? Isaiah?"

Emery felt her face heat. She cleared her throat.

"Wait, what? Are you dating him?"

"Sort of?"

Lacey shook her head. "And what about Nash?"

She threw her hands up. "Why does everyone think there's something with Nash? We don't talk, and if we do, nice words don't flow."

Lacey grinned. "But he's so delicious. How can you not think about Nash? Besides, he's always around. Haven't you both done every rodeo together for like the last two years?"

"Something like that. But we're both chasing prize money. So that's why we're always together. He's going to be there when we arrive. It's good timing, because he's hurting with a concussion and needs to take a four-week break."

"Ooh, so he needs someone like me to keep him company?"

"Exactly." Emery laughed, thrilled that her situation was working out exactly as planned.

"Awesome. I'll take on as much of your stuff as I can so you can nurse our dear Nashy Nash back to health."

Emery's mouth dropped open. "No, that's not what I meant."

Lacey waved her hand. "I'll take care of it."

"You don't understand. Some of my stuff I cannot hand off. Like I'm actually riding tonight."

"Great. We'll sit in the stands and watch you. Sister, don't stress. I'll earn my keep in whatever ways I can around this place." She flipped the visor down and checked her teeth. "Is there anyone nearby I could explore?"

"What about your butler at the airport?" Emery laughed.

"He's not my type. Did you see how sculpted he was? It's like he'd shaved his whole body or something."

Emery grinned. "I don't know if any of the rodeo hands are your type. But I'm sure you'll know soon enough. Let's listen to some real music."

Lacey cranked up the tunes, and just like old times when the two of them had nothing and no one else but each other, they sang at the top of their lungs to every song that came on the radio. By the time they arrived at the rodeo grounds in Mesquite, Emery's voice was hoarse. "Lacey, I needed that."

She laughed. "Me too." A flash of pain crossed her face.

Emery reached for her hand. "Tell me all about it."

"I will. Later. Right now, I'm seeing a hottie standing there with nothing to do but hang out with the Banks sisters." She laughed loud and long and then rolled down her window, cheering. "Mesquite, Texas! It's time to partay!" Her hand waved everywhere. Then she ducked her head in. "Honk your horn."

Emery shook her head.

"Oh come on, honk your horn. We need an entrance."

But Emery turned off the car before Lacey could reach the steering wheel.

"Let's get you unloaded."

Lacey leapt out of the truck and ran to Nash. "It's my favorite cowboy!" She flung her arms around his neck and clung to him, rocking back and forth so long, Emery was about to call her off.

Nash lifted a hand in Emery's direction and winked. "Well aren't you looking fine, Miss Lacey Banks?"

"I certainly am. Thank you for noticing." She spun around. "And I'm here to keep you company. Someone told me you're gonna be lonely and out of commission for a while."

"She's mostly right. I'm also doing my good bit of chores."

"Oh yeah, me too. I told Emery to give me everything she can while I'm here."

Nash looked her up and down—one quick assessment and Emery knew he'd figured accurately just how many chores Lacey was gonna be doing.

But maybe she'd surprise them all.

"Let's get you unloaded." As soon as he lifted the cover, he whistled. "You got space for all this?"

Emery winced. "I figured we could use the storage."

"And my place." He thumbed it toward his trailer. "You can use the back bedroom for whatever you like."

Emery opened her mouth to let Nash off the hook, but

Lacey wrapped her hands around his bicep. "Thank you. I moved out of my apartment. This is all I own in the world. You should have seen what I threw away." She made a point of measuring his arm. "My word, you've got huge arms. Have you seen this muscle?"

She laughed, showing Emery, who could only grin and shrug. "Yep. I've seen it."

Nash gently unentangled himself and then hefted the largest suitcase. "Which trailer? Mine or yours?"

"Oh, that sounds so devilish. Too bad I know you would only direct those kinds of comments elsewhere." Lacey giggled.

Emery and Nash ignored that comment, Emery not even looking in his direction. The next bag was more medium sized. "Oh, that goes wherever I go," Lacey told Nash. "Can Emery show you where to put that in her place?" Lacey made a show of diving into her carry-on for something.

"Right this way," Emery said. "Oh, that reminds me. Can you stand outside with the crank while I push the expansion open?"

"Oh sure. We have one at home that does this. I know right where you need me," Nash replied.

Lacey snorted and Emery wanted to squirt her with water. She hurried up into the trailer. Then she called out the window, "I'm pushing the button now."

"Got it."

The trailer beeped, and the back end started moving outward. It was slow but steady, and Nash must have put the crank in at the right moment and guided the mechanisms, because pretty soon, the space was unfolded and the bed visible.

Nash stepped inside.

And the space became much smaller.

He moved toward the expansion. "Can I check it out?"

"Sure." Emery's voice squeaked, but she followed him as if nothing were wreaking havoc on her peace of mind.

"Sometimes there are some glitches." He pointed to a spot that looked like it hadn't completely unfolded. He pushed it with his hands, the muscles on his arms becoming more defined, closing a crack in her wall. "There we go."

She tore her eyes away from his bicep to his face, nodding. "Thank you."

He placed the luggage on the bed. "This is nice—almost new looking in here."

"It really is. I hardly use it nowadays. We were gifted the whole thing by Billy when we first started on. He used it for the help, he said, but I wonder now if he was just helping out a couple ladies who had nowhere else to go."

"Sounds like you also worked really hard for him. And look, now you're one of his top racers."

Emery dipped her head, not really sure how true all that was. It was difficult always living on the charity of others. Did she ever deserve any of it? Had she worked hard enough? And the real question: Was she any good? The sponsorship was sort of proving that for her. They'd never pick her unless they thought she was one of the best in the world. That was something. But then Isaiah had started hanging around. And she doubted herself once more.

All she could do was nod to Nash, and then follow him back out of the home.

"The other big ones go to your place, and all the rest of these smaller ones need to find a spot in ours." Lacey picked up three of the small ones. "I'll start unpacking." She stepped up on the first stair. "It's good to be home." And then she disappeared inside.

"I'll help with these." Emery hefted the closest larger piece.

"You sure? I can get it," Nash said.

She was sure. He'd seen inside her trailer. She wanted a peek inside his.

CHAPTER 7

$\mathcal{A}$s soon as Emery stepped inside his trailer, Nash knew he'd never be able to sleep in that space again. Her scent of strawberries filled the air, mixed with the clean smell of her soap. Everywhere her gaze moved, he followed. The space was clean. He hoped it smelled all right.

She stopped in front of the latest picture of his family. "The Dawson family legacy." She lifted up the small frame. "Would you look at that?" She held it close, like she was trying to see each face.

"We're growing. My brothers are all having kids like crazy. Going home is like being attacked by the kid brigade." He laughed, but he loved it. "It's part of the reason I'm working on the children's center in Willow Creek."

She turned and rested a hip on his counter. Seeing her in his living space was doing things to him. Things like wanting to place a hand on her hip right there, tugging it closer to him. He leaned up on that same counter next to her. After all, there just wasn't that much space in the trailer to begin with.

She smiled. "I'm interested in the children's center. What are you planning?"

"I'm working on it with Grace. She's my eldest niece and we're close. I'd like to donate it to her once it's up and running—a way to add more to the Dawson family brand, and to give her an income."

"That's . . ." Emery seemed to have difficulty talking, and she looked away, some kind of emotion on her face.

"What did I do? I'm sorry." He leaned forward, trying to catch her expression.

But she turned back, moisture in her eyes. "No, it's not you. You're awesome. I'm just sitting here having a little bit of a pity party, or maybe it's just an appreciation party. You're good to your people, Nash. I respect that."

He thumbed it over toward Lacey in her trailer. "And look at you with yours. We're more alike than you think, Emery Banks."

She laughed. "I never said we weren't alike." She nudged him with her shoulder. "I said you were getting under my skin."

His mouth lifted in a slow, long smile of pure enjoyment. Then he side-stepped close enough that their shoulders didn't just bump, they stayed pressed together. And their hips. And their arms. "I think about you being under my skin all the time. But I don't think our definitions of the phrase mean the same thing."

She turned to him, their faces close, her eyes reading him, always reading. The woman would not trust him for a long time. He saw that. But he could earn her trust, starting with some help with her sister.

"I'm afraid to ask what your definition means." Her words were almost a whisper and a dare.

He reached out, running his fingers along her hairline, brushing away any strands that blocked his view of her eyes. "I'll tell you anytime."

She closed her eyes, her soft smile one of the most inviting things Nash had ever seen. He wanted to cup her face and gently press his lips to hers once, twice, just a test to see if she would like it or slug him.

But she opened them again and nodded to herself, stepping forward off his counter. "Thank you for this. I have no idea if she'll need all this or just need a place to keep it." She shrugged. "I don't know how long she's staying or what she'll want. I have the rodeo tonight. I've got to run Stargazer through the route—"

"I know. Rodeo guy here, remember? I'll take care of it. Lacey and I are going to get along just fine."

But Emery tilted her head, suddenly looking suspicious. "Not too fine." She held up a finger.

"Don't be ridiculous. I can't even begin this conversation. Go. Let's get out of here before I forget myself."

She laughed, but then paused so that he almost bumped into her on their way out. He reached up a hand to steady his balance. She stood almost inside an embrace, their bodies close enough that he felt the warmth from hers and breathed in the fruity, clean smell that he hoped lingered after she left. She turned her head, catching his gaze with hers again. "Maybe I want you to forget yourself sometimes."

His eye brows shot up, and this time, his hand did rest at her hip.

She relaxed even closer to him.

Lacey banged open the door. Her eyes widened, and she turned around and walked out again. "Sorry!" she called back to them.

Emery groaned, and basically ran after her sister, not looking back.

She wanted him to forget himself sometimes? What exactly did that mean? Sometimes? Not always. Obviously not when she was mad at him, which was most of the time. He ran a hand through his hair. And then he grinned. This had to be progress. A step in the right direction. She'd admitted something. And let him get close, real close—close enough to know she might want to kiss him.

Nash almost did a great, big cowboy yeehaw right there in his trailer, but decided against it when Lacey's laugh carried so easily over to him from inside theirs.

It was a weird kind of torture to park himself right next door to Emery, but he liked being close. And he saw her more often that way.

The smell of strawberries lingered. He breathed in deeply, his gaze following everywhere she had been. It was nice to have her in here with him, real nice—the kind of nice that he'd like to repeat a few more times.

But the chores wouldn't complete themselves. And now he'd be trying to do them with Lacey tagging along. He snorted. That woman could use a few hours in the hot sun, getting her hands dirty.

Today, they would be heading over to the arena to get all the animals ready for tonight. Since Nash wouldn't be riding, he'd offered to prep with the bullfighters. And since they wouldn't let him anywhere near the space during an actual rodeo, he would be working background help for the rest of the show.

He brushed his teeth again, spiffed up his hair, and then stepped out of his trailer.

Lacey and Emery were standing close, having some kind

of discussion, and it didn't look like anyone was agreeing with anything.

He cleared his throat.

They both turned, the fire of a contest shooting daggers in his direction.

He held up his hands. "Just wondering if anyone was heading to the arena, 'cause I got space in my truck." They could walk over, but they were running later than usual, and the truck was useful to have over there.

Lacey huffed. "Sounds like I am." She shouldered a drawstring bag and marched past him toward the truck.

Emery met Nash's gaze and shrugged, looking like an apology was ready to come pouring out of her mouth.

But he shook his head. "Good luck tonight. I'll be running errands or mucking out stables, or maybe I'll put on a clown outfit." He frowned. "Not that I'm bitter."

"You can be bitter." She lifted her chin toward Lacey. "Thank you."

"You're welcome. This is gonna be the sweet part of a day full of the other."

She nodded.

"You signed with Bunson yet?"

She shook her head, a flash of concern crossing her face. "Isaiah keeps saying he has the paperwork, but he called me this morning to say he'd not be bringing it by until tomorrow." She hugged herself, rubbing both her arms. Nash wished to step in and offer more hugging from his direction, but now was not the time.

"That's good, though, right?" he asked.

"I guess so. I mean, yeah, of course."

"But?"

She laughed, waving her fingers in the air. "I'm being

ridiculous. But I'll keep worrying about things until I have it signed in front of me. Isaiah wants to go out tonight."

Nash stiffened. "But he doesn't want to sign until tomorrow?" Was he dangling the contract in front of her, trying to get dates out of the woman? Or more?

"Doesn't want to mix business with pleasure." She shrugged again.

Nash had other thoughts, but he gritted his teeth and kept them to himself. No guarantee he would do as much if Isaiah came within ten feet of him. "So, you're a thing now? Going out twice this weekend?" He tried to act casual, but his voice, his stance, everything about him was accusatory right now.

"We're what we were before." Emery crossed her arms. "We're talking. Dating." She turned away. "I don't need to explain my personal life to you. Thank you. For helping out. But this stuff is off limits." She held up her hands.

"Understood." He stood taller. "You still want a ride over?" He indicated Lacey in his front seat, applying lipstick to impress the stock.

"Yeah, let me grab my gear bag." She hurried back up the steps into her trailer, and Nash wanted to kick himself, keep razzing her, and lay a fist into Isaiah's face all at the same time.

When he got into the car, he was greeted by the overly friend face of Emery's sister. "Hey now, let's go have some fun today." Lacey wrapped her hands around his bicep again. And with Emery not watching, it just wasn't as fun anymore. Her smile was sugar sweet and almost alluring.

"You don't have to do that, you know." He eyed her hands on his arm until she released him.

"Do what?" She dabbed both sides of her lips with a finger.

"Reach and smile and flirt." He shrugged. "Guys will like you even if you're just sitting there. Being yourself."

Her mouth dropped open, and she closed it again. "Well, I'm not trying to get you to like me, not like that. You're Emery's, plain as day. But I'd like to have a little fun. This is me being myself." She pouted, and then ran a few fingers up his arm. "You're so stiff and unhappy today. You need to relax."

Nash shook her off. "There. That. You are sending all the wrong signals. Try sitting back with all your body parts in your own space and telling me something about yourself or your plans today. Let's have a normal conversation."

"Wow, you're a barrel of laughs this morning." Lacey pulled out her phone.

"What are you doing?"

"Just seeing if there's anywhere in the world I can be besides right here with you."

Alarm bells started to ring. He was supposed to be helping Emery by keeping Lacey here and happy. "No. Come on. I'm just fired up about the contract not being signed and sponsorships for Emery, and sometimes I want to slam my fist in a wall."

"And I interrupted an almost kiss." She grinned. "I can see why you might be a little testy with me right now."

He was about to deny it, but then he tilted his head and took a chance. "Yes! I'd like to have words with you for barging in right then. Any other moment would have been fine, but then? You had to choose right then?" He moved the truck into reverse. "Is she coming?"

Her trailer door opened and Emery ran out with gear over her shoulder. Her hair was pulled back from her long, slender neck, and a tight-fitting shirt hugged her down to her jeans. He looked away.

"I'll let her in first. How's that for apologies?" Lacey winked.

"You're well on your way to redeeming yourself, little lady." He smiled. They might get on well after all.

But Emery huffed while climbing in. "You have to make me slide all the way across? Really, Lacey, we're not kids anymore. Give a girl the door." She slid two heaving motions until she was almost pressed up against Nash, which he quite enjoyed, but Emery seemed to not notice.

Lacey flashed him a brief, sympathetic something before Emery looked from one to the other. "What?"

Nash widened his eyes and then began backing up the truck. "What nothing. You ready?"

"Yep."

He backed them up and then started up the long gravel road, which winded around the arena property to the front gate, where he could park his truck. Walking was closer, but driving was often quicker. Emery didn't say much. Lacey said nothing. And Nash started and stopped about five conversations in his head before giving up and turning on the radio.

His leg was pressed up against Emery's, but even that didn't soften the tense feelings between them.

When he pulled to a stop, the gravel cloud billowed up around them. He turned to Emery. "Good luck today. I'll be getting the animals prepped and checking the arena. If you want, I can give Stargazer some extra attention."

Her shoulders relaxed a moment. "Sure, that would be great. I'll be walking her and doing a quick ride myself. But yeah, she could use a friendly face back there. It's a big day for us."

He put a hand on her knee. It was meant to be a warm gesture, somewhat comforting even, but his reaction was not warm, comforting, or even friendly. Even his toes wanted more than that quick pressure on her leg. He pulled his hand away. "I wanted to say, it's going to be great. You'll be great." He cleared his throat and then opened the truck door. He stepped his boot down on the dusty gravel road and then rotated his shoulders. Today was going to be a long day.

Lacey stepped up beside him. "What are we doing first, boss?" Her nose wrinkled and then she fanned her face. "Is it always hot, dusty, and smelly?"

"You're at the rodeo, darling, that's what we live for." Nash sniffed his shirt. "It's my perfume." He wiggled his eyebrows, and she rolled hers.

But he rested his arm across her shoulders. "Come on, Lace. You've done this before. Remember your roots."

"My roots shoveled a lot of manure."

"Perfect, because you and me? We're on stall duty."

But to his surprise, she just nodded. "Just point me to the shovel."

Emery grinned at him, and the three of them made their way through the arena's front doors.

It was safe to say that not every eye looked in their direction when they walked through the doors, but every male eye did.

Whether they were checking out Emery or Lacey, Nash couldn't tell, but something about all that male attention toward the Banks sisters sent his chin up and his fists clenching. "Why they gotta check you out the second you walk in the door?" He grunted.

And then Lacey laughed. "Oh, cowboy. We can take care of ourselves. Bristle down. Me and Em, we've been handling this crowd our whole lives." She winked and then sent a three-finger wave toward Eric, who was priming the popcorn machine.

"Do I need to worry about you getting into trouble with our concessions guy?" Nash asked.

"Not unless you have a problem with me smelling like buttered popcorn." She laughed. "Relax." This time, she didn't run a hand down his arm, and he felt a bit better about that.

"I'll do my best. Today's not promising to be the relaxing kind."

They separated at the dirt. Emery went to go prepare to actually participate in the rodeo, and Nash, he led Lacey around to the shovels. They inspected the stalls. So early in the morning, everything was still clean. All the animals had feed. Everyone was doing a job. Really, the background work of running a rodeo had been functioning without Nash for years. There was no reason why they would need him or Lacey now.

"Maybe we should go watch?" He stepped up to the fence rails to look out across the arena.

One of the managers rushed by. "Nash, and you." He pointed to Lacey. "We could use some riders in the parade."

He leapt off the railing, Lacey not far behind. "That's more like it," he said.

"Can you ride?" She hurried to match his long strides with her much shorter legs.

He tried not to be too rude with the look he gave her.

She laughed. "With your head? Can you ride while you have a concussion?"

"As long as I don't get jostled around, the doc should be

happy as peach pie." He winked, the new energy to actually be up on an animal, in front of the rodeo crowd, giving him a whole new happy perspective on life.

"Well, aren't you full of roses and sunshine." Lacey laughed again, but her steps were equally as quick, and they hurried to the lineup to see what needed to be ridden.

CHAPTER 8

*Journal Challenge Entry: Because I've been focused on goodness
and grace and help from Heaven, I've been happier. I've been able
to really enjoy my sister here with me and can see that there might
be a reason she is here, a bigger reason than getting kicked out of
her apartment. Also, for some reason, when I'm reading the Bible, I
get along with Nash better.*

*E*mery hurried to her horse. Too much confusion
was interrupting normal thought in her brain, and
before she made any decision ruled by emotion, she had to
center herself. She needed Stargazer. Her steps quickened.

Seeing Lacey with Nash did good and bad things to her.
She sighed. It made him feel like family. And she yearned for
that. The three of them in his truck, going to work on the
rodeo. It was too familiar. And then his hand on her knee.
She shivered with pleasure. That was too good, too much,
and not allowed. She was not going to fall for Nash Dawson.
Who was she kidding? She'd loved him for years. But she
also couldn't stand him. And those kinds of relationships

didn't work out in the end. Not usually. Besides, she had Isaiah.

Two dates with the man. She'd not promised anything, but he was assuming they were going out to eat tonight after the rodeo. And he was taking her someplace nice tomorrow night. And then they would talk contracts Sunday.

She knew what got Nash all in an uproar. She was beginning to suspect Isaiah too. But at the same time, he was a perfectly respectable guy. And he was offering her all her dreams on a platter. She was not stupid. She'd go out with the guy, but she had her limits.

And besides, maybe some kind of spark would light up and she could find it in her to be attracted to the man. He wasn't unattractive. Lots of women wanted to be in her boots.

But she was just so dang distracted by Nash. And now he was giving her attention. An odd sort of attention. Watching her sister, storing their luggage, the physical clues . . . she didn't know what to make of it. He'd never asked her out. Didn't really socialize with her. But as she thought about the past four months of rodeo, he was always there. And she realized, subconsciously, she'd come to count on that. She turned to him. Even with her sister. They had these conversations where they'd get real for about five minutes and then start razzing each other for the next twenty. But those five minutes had added up over time.

What did Nash want?

What was he afraid of?

She had no idea. Except, of course, they both wanted money. But why did he?

At last, she stood in front of Stargazer. She breathed in the horse's smells, stepped inside the stall with her, and wrapped her arms around her neck. "There's my good girl." With a cheek pressed to the horse's flank, she started humming. Stargazer nuzzled her and bumped her leg. "Easy, girl. I'm just having one of those days." The responding nicker almost made her think the horse had learned to understand.

Maybe she did. Stargazer bumped her in the stomach, and then nibbled at her shirt. She wasn't supposed to, but it was the closest thing to a kiss the horse could give right then and Emery took it. "Thank you, girl. We have a lot of work to do today. You ready to fly?" She kissed her soft nose. "You ready to fly round those barrels like no one else has ever seen?" Emery grinned. "'Cause I am. And one day, we'll make enough money to get out of this place. To settle in our own house, to let you run free. Maybe even breed a couple." She gave Stargazer one extra squeeze, full of promise. "Someday."

Isaiah appeared out of nowhere and leaned his forearms against her stall door, making her jump.

Stargazer shifted and pawed the ground.

"Whoa there." Emery placed a hand over the star on the horse's head. "Easy."

"How's my favorite barrel-racing duo today?"

"We're doing great! Just checking in with her. She seems warm, ready. She's had her morning feed and water. We'll take her out and walk and run her in a bit."

"Good news. And the rider?" Isaiah smiled. The man's smile could melt many a heart not made of stone. But Emery's seemed to be of the unmelting kind.

She returned his smile with a genuine one of her own. The man cared, and he was interested in her. That was gratifying. She should be grateful. And she liked him. What was there not to like?

"I'm well. Lacey came into town today."

"I heard. She's making quite a stir with all the men around here." He laughed. "She's a looker like her sister, though I prefer this variety of Banks." He winked. "How long will she be here?"

"I'm not sure. She's needing a new home, so I'm a stopover until she gets her feet underneath her again."

"Bunson is coming at a good time, then."

"Yes. It really is."

Isaiah nodded. "Well, I'm glad to hear it, and happy I played my small part. Sometimes all it takes is a healthy recommendation."

"Thank you again for that." Would she be thanking him her whole life? How much of this did she deserve really?

"I know good talent and a healthy career when I see one. I just did the due diligence and passed on what I've seen. But anyway, neither here nor there. We have a date with the best ice cream house in Texas tonight. You still up for it?"

"You bet. That sounds so nice right now."

"We can celebrate your first-place ribbon."

Emery laughed. But he seemed serious.

"I'll try for a personal best. This rodeo pulls in some of the long-time ranking stars. I think the best we can promise is winning block. Not certain we can win out over Rising Tide. They're the reigning champions and hold the record. They're going to be here today too."

"A Bunson rider can handle that kind of competition. We choose the best in the business, and that's why we chose you. Remember that."

She was sure he meant to be encouraging, to help motivate or strengthen her, but all she felt was pressure—a horrible, winding, tightening pressure. All at once, her breath struggled to enter and leave her body.

"But I'll leave you to it. Looks like you need to get in the zone." Isaiah wiggled his fingers like he knew what he was talking about, like *she* even knew what he was talking about. "And I'm in the way. Good luck. I'll be up in the announcer box this time, but know I'm cheering you on."

"Thank you." Her smile was weak. She felt weak.

Stargazer nudged her again.

"I don't even know. What are we doing here, little lady, just what?"

Emery changed into costume, dressed up Stargazer, adding a braid and a ribbon to the horse's mane, and then got ready for the early parade-practice lineup. All the contestants had a chance to run through the parade and then take their time on the arena dirt to help the animals acclimate to their new environment.

She hadn't seen Nash or Lacey and hadn't given them too much thought, but now that she was done with most of the prep work, she wondered how they'd used their time.

And then her answer came in a loud ruckus at the end of the hall.

Laughter and cheers followed an approaching duo. Nash and Lacey, dressed as the parade boss, both of them, were riding side by side in full red, white, and blue patriotic garb. And Lacey could not look happier. That woman needed attention, and lots of it.

Nash, on the other hand, looked bored.

And then his eyes met Emery's, and did not leave.

They paraded backstage, down the long hallway, making their way to the front of the line, but as they passed Emery,

Nash bowed, his hand dramatically raising out behind him. Lacey waved wildly. "Emery! Look at us!"

She laughed. "I see. This is way better than mucking stalls."

"You know it. But I'll be doing that later." She waved her manicured hands and then sat up taller. "I miss this, you know?"

"I know." Emery lifted her leg up on the stirrup and swung herself up into the saddle. They waited until almost the whole place had lined up behind those two, and then she joined them at the rear of the processional.

The announcer's voice came out over the speaker. "And now we will do our parade run-through. After this dress rehearsal, please follow the order you're in for the animals' run-through if you wish to have one."

Emery would. And she'd need the barrels set up, but she'd already arranged for such a thing to happen.

The parade and her run-through went well. Isaiah even made some kind of comment in the mic when she was finished, which earned some chuckles from the fighters who were getting ready at the fences. They were about to bring out the bulls to let them take a turn around the space and remind them to head back into their stalls for food and water.

Emery lugged the first barrel backstage and came back out for the second.

Nash rolled it in.

"Where did you come from?" She smiled. "Thanks."

"Just fitting in where I can. There's really nothing for me to do." His eyes filled with a pained desperation that she immediately understood.

"I think I heard that the bulls were giving everyone some trouble. They're out next."

"Oh, that's great news." He laughed. "I guess." He ran a hand through his hair. "Honestly, I don't think I'm going to survive the next four weeks."

"I hear ya. But they won't all be in Mesquite. Aren't we traveling to Oregon next weekend?"

His eyes clouded, and he shook his head. "Sounds like you are. Congratulations. That's a huge show. You should earn a lot of prize money there."

She felt the sharp pang of disappointment stronger than she would have thought. A rodeo without Nash? "Yeah, thanks. As long as I can keep winning. Even if I place. It all depends if Rising Tide shows up. And I've heard she's going. She's here tonight."

Nash shook his head. "Don't let her mess with your head. You've got to be fast and balanced, and it's all about you and Stargazer. She has no business being anywhere near that real estate in your mind."

"I know that," Emery snapped. And then she amended her tone. "I've just got a lot riding on this tonight, I think."

"Is Isaiah still putting on the pressure? Acting like the deal isn't signed?" Nash's face was an unreadable mask of quiet.

"Not really, no."

"But there's that sense." He shook his head. "It's uncool what he's doing."

"Maybe, or maybe he just wanted to get to know a rider who also happens to be a sponsorship contender."

"Recipient now."

She dipped her head in acknowledgment, hoping that was true. Until that contract was signed, she couldn't feel completely at ease.

Her phone rang, and she smiled. Then she lifted it to her ear. "Milly Dawson, how are you?" She grinned at Nash, whose expression was priceless.

"My mom?" He pointed.

Emery nodded.

"And she regularly calls you? Like you're using her first name?"

Emery rolled her eyes and nodded again. "I hear you. That sounds wonderful. It's the one weekend I don't have a rodeo scheduled. Put me on the list. I'm coming to Willow Creek."

Nash's mouth dropped. "What?"

She turned to him. "Yes, Nash is right here. Yes, you can." She offered her phone. "Your mother wants to talk to you." She couldn't help the laugh that bubbled up inside.

He took her phone. "Hey, Mama. How you doing?"

"I'm doing just fine, son, just fine. Actually, I'm laughing to myself over here wondering what you're thinking."

"I'm not thinking anything. Just working the background on a rodeo I should be winning." He frowned.

"And still helping out our Emery?"

"Our? Eh. Yes, I am." His eyes flit to her and then away.

"Just wanted you to know, it's confirmed. Billy's doing a rodeo out here in Willow Creek. And it's back-to-back with the national one coming to Ashville the next weekend. Emery's coming. I told her Lacey is welcome. I expect you'll be home as well?"

"Sure, Mama. I can make it work."

"I don't think you need to be riding it."

"I'll be riding both. There's a lot of prize money there. And I gotta start earning my way here. Doc will clear me."

"But he won't be happy about it."

He sighed, aware that he had an audience. And that he was still talking on Emery's phone. "Thanks for letting me know, Ma. I'll get on their docket right away."

"And you'll take good care of my Emery?"

"Yours? Uh, yes. I'll do that."

"Thank you. You're a good son. And there's a reason you came last."

"I know, Ma. Okay, I gotta run and get this whole thing moving."

"And you're done taking orders from your mother."

"Never done. Thank you."

"You're welcome."

He handed the phone back to Emery. "I'm not sure how I feel about my mom scheduling you for our hometown rodeo before she scheduled me."

"I can't explain it except she needs some barrel racers?" She shrugged. "She asked for Lacey to come too, to help work booths. She's a good woman, your mother—all you Dawsons." Emery winked. "Even their youngest now and then."

Nash hmphed. "Now and then, she says. If I don't get back out there soon, I'll be good for no one."

"You're doing great now. Love the costume." She snorted and then giggled, and she resisted covering her mouth with one hand because that would add to the ridiculous giggling, but it was just too funny. And at his expense. "Look, we should get out of here, go somewhere without all the distraction." Had she just asked him out? She wished really badly to take it all back in, reel it close like a fishing hook, wrap it up, and attach it to the rod. That should not have been said.

"You mean, like an ice cream after the show tonight?" His eyes flashed at her.

"Well, no."

"Since you're already doing that. With Isaiah. Right. You mean like right now, while we're trying to get ready?"

"No. Look, Nash, I get it. Sorry. It just sounded nice. I spoke without thinking. I'm not trying to rub in your pain here. I'm trying to help." She looked away and then spurred her horse forward. She was so done with him.

But he hurried up at her side. "I'm a jerk."

She laughed, surprised, but didn't respond.

"No really, I know I'm the worst company. Have a good rodeo. I'll be cheering you on from the west stands with Lacey. There's nothing else for me to do here, and I'm bored and it's driving me crazy."

"Take Lacey out dancing." She hurried to say the words before she could take them back. "She's a hoot. It will take your mind off."

He nodded and then tilted her head. "You sure you're not trying to set me up here?"

"No. I'm not. I'm really not." She stared him down. "But I'm busy, so . . ."

"So you're sending your sister to clean up the sick lap dog?" He shook his head. "I'll be just fine. Besides, I think she has a date with the concessions guy."

Emery smiled.

Nash tipped his hat. "I'll be seeing you."

She watched him go, her thoughts distracted by too many other things to also be concerned with a moody cowboy, even if it was Nash.

Until she saw a pretty blonde run to him and hug him like she had good news.

Was that Dakota?

She knew they were close, real close—the kind of close

that made her jealous. Why couldn't she run into Nash's arms and be excited about good news? She tore her eyes away. They just weren't like that.

Lacey rode up. "Hey, you gonna knock down any barrels?"

"Nope."

"That's what I like to hear." She held out her fist for some knocks. "Rodeo is a good life. I'd forgotten about the people, the thrill, the hype. I see why you're still here."

"The money." Emery shook her head. "We need the prize money. I've been saving, and we're almost there."

Lacey looked away like she wasn't listening. "Who's the overly happy blonde?"

Emery didn't bother faking ignorance. "Dakota."

Lacey nodded. "I'll take care of it." She clucked, and she and the horse sauntered away.

"Don't take care of it," Emery called over her shoulder.

But Lacey didn't respond.

When it was finally time to ride, Emery was a ball of nerves. Stargazer pranced in place. Nothing felt right.

Rising Tide rode out right before she did. Her rider, Trish, flipped her hair in Emery's direction once, but that was all the interaction they'd had. Emery had tried to give her space, and she didn't want to mess with her own head. So when Trish came tearing back in after what looked like a near perfect run, Emery could only feel her options seeping away. She had known winners' block was what she could expect. She was practical about her money-making plans. It was just Isaiah who had put the pressure on and made her feel like if she didn't win first place, she'd be letting down her sponsor. And she supposed she would. But that just wasn't who she was. Everyone knew and expected Trish to win.

And that was okay. Emery was still earning enough off her second- and third-place spots to reach her dreams with a little more patience.

Trish laughed as she circled around behind Emery. "Good luck out there. It's tough on the horses who can't cut quite as sharp an angle as my Rising Tide here." She clucked and then guided her horse down the hall, presumably toward her stables.

But Emery's blood burst to flames. "Did you hear that Stargazer?" She patted her on the flank. "She's laying down some kind of challenge. Can't cut sharp angles?" Emery squeezed her thighs and Stargazer jumped forward to their starting point, dancing in place and then pausing, perched, ready to spring.

Emery leaned forward, weight off, gripping the reins. Everything went quiet expect for Stargazer's breathing. She used the sensation of in and out to focus her ride, let it center her thoughts. She felt the horse's breathing under her legs. They were one. When the signal went off, she and Stargazer tore out onto the dirt like never before. She raced around the first barrel, wobbling it a smidge, but it stayed upright, circled the next with the tiniest fraction of space, ran to the next set, repeated an excellent circle, and then raced as fast as she'd ever seen her horse race, back into the darkness off the arena floor.

The crowd leapt to its feet.

Everything came back into focus for Emery. The announcer shouted, "And that is a new world record! Hats off to our own Emery Banks for beating the last world record, formerly held by the previous rider-horse duo Jolene Walker and Cinnamon. Come on out here, Emery!"

She patted her horse and leaned forward, hugging her. "Good show, girl. We did it."

And then they walked back out into the arena.

The crowds went crazy. Everyone was on their feet. Her eyes found Nash and Lacey. Her sister was going cray. She jumped up and down, throwing her arms around Nash while she screamed. Nash tipped his hat to Emery.

And then Emery lifted a hand to the stands, to all the shouting, happy faces. This was her home. This was her life. And she'd done it. She saluted the announcer box and Stargazer went down on one knee in a mock bow.

Everyone ate it up. She did a quick circle around with her horse, showing off just a bit. Stargazer tossed her head and neighed once, even. Emery laughed and then cried and then laughed again while she circled her horse, catching her breath. "Good girl. That's my Stargazer," she said over and over.

CHAPTER 9

ash could not be more proud of Emery. She ran a barrel race almost flawlessly. He'd never seen it run so well. And to now hold the world record—that was something. He stood with the rest of them and laughed with Lacey when Stargazer took her own bow.

"That's right! You deserve it, Star!" Lacey shouted over the top of most people around them.

People started shouting out the horse's name, and then a chant began—"Stargazer," over and over—and Nash chanted right along with them.

Emery raised her hand and blew a kiss to the stands.

Men all around Nash reached up to catch it and began hooting and hollering enough that he wanted to step in between them and Emery. And then the announcer clicked on. "Let's hear it one more time for Mesquite's own Emery Banks!"

Everyone cheered like crazy again and then began to settled back down in their seats. And then an annoying voice took the microphone. Isaiah. "And I'm sorry to say it, gentleman, but I have it on good authority that our Miss Banks is taken."

Lacey gasped.

Emery stiffened. Nash could see her stance change from where he sat.

Some men in the crowd booed, but mostly, they'd moved on. Emery left the arena.

Lacey stood. "I'm going to her."

He followed. "Me too."

She laughed.

"What?" he asked.

"Well, what are you going to do?"

"I don't know. See if she's okay?"

"Stake your claim?" Lacey raised an eyebrow and shook her head.

And then he wasn't sure what he was going to do, because now that she mentioned it, he looked at things, and knew he was really going to stake his claim, plain as day. But what claim was he staking? Did he plan on taking her out? Did he want a woman in his life? No, he most definitely did not want a woman in his life, officially. But Emery was in his life. He'd slowly but surely made her a part of everything he did, including bunking down right next to her at every arena.

"I'm coming," he said.

Lacey shrugged and led the way out of the stands.

When they finally reached her horse, Stargazer was watered, fed, and brushed down, but no Emery was in sight.

"Where is she?" Lacey turned with a huff.

"Maybe she ran? So mad at Isaiah, she took off?" A man could hope.

But Eric the concessions guy called over to them while cleaning out his booth. "Nah, she left with him. They looked pretty happy about it even after he was claiming her all over the announcements." He shrugged. "I think they went to Tap N' Grill. Good dancing tonight." He glanced up at Lacey more than once, but she didn't notice. And Nash wasn't about to point it out, because he needed Lacey himself.

"Hey, wanna go to Tap N' Grill, you know, to get a burger?" he asked.

"And a beer?"

"Sure, whatever you want."

"And some dancing?"

"Yep."

"You're on. I don't even need to go freshen up. Let's go spy on my sister."

He opened his mouth to deny everything that might have been going through her mind, but gave up before he even formulated a sentence. He was spying and getting ready to intervene if necessary. Plain as day, true as the sun rose, and they both knew it.

"All right, then. Let's get my truck."

As they passed Eric, Lacey let her hand trail along his countertop. "You could meet us there."

His face lit up like a floodlight, and he started scrubbing that booth like his life depended on it.

"Wow." Nash gave her an appraising look. "That didn't take long."

"For what?"

"To win him over."

He expected some kind of arrogant, flippant comment, but instead her face colored pink and she looked away. "Nah. He's just being nice."

"Ho ho! Does Lacey have a crush?" He nudged her with his shoulder.

"Stop. I don't have a crush. He's just a nice guy. I don't know too many of those."

They hopped in the truck, and he headed toward the highway that would take them to Tap N' Grill. After a few miles of comfortable silence, Lacey turned toward him. "I don't even know what to do to keep a nice guy." She shrugged. "Or any guy."

"What's the longest relationship you've ever had?"

"Really? A couple months. I just . . . get bored." She fiddled with her shirt. "And I've never really had anyone but Emery. She never gives up on me, no matter what I do. No one else is like that. It's easier not to test them, you know? So I don't get too attached and they walk off. I don't think I'm the easiest person to live with."

Nash tried to gather his thoughts for a minute. "That was a lot to unpack, you know. Everything you just said. But I get it. I think to some degree, every single one of us is afraid of commitment and rejection. So that makes you normal. And then the other part about walking off before you can get hurt—that sounds like self-preservation to me."

Lacey held up her fist. "So basically, you're the same as me?"

He bumped her back. "I think in some ways, yes, I am."

"Why don't you have a girlfriend?" She brought her leg up on the truck bench and adjusted herself so that she was comfortably facing him with her seat belt on.

So she was settling in, trying to get the deets on him. He'd be smart to remember she was Emery's sister.

"I'll trade my deets for some intel on Emery."

She nodded. "Done."

"That easy? You would tell on your sister?"

"Not telling on her. I won't say anything she'd be too

82

terribly displeased to hear about, and I definitely won't embarrass her. But I'm on team hashtag Nashery. So I'm going to do what I can to get you two together."

"I like that. Nashery. Or Emenash."

Lacey waved her hand. "Either one. So spill."

"For a long time, I just didn't really have time for a girl-friend and no interest. I was doing a rodeo circuit that took me to a bunch of regional shows, one after another, and the money was mediocre, so I had to do a lot to stay afloat. I had dates, things to do for one weekend here or there, but no one who would want to have this kind of life. It just isn't good for girlfriends or wives."

She nodded. "I can see that."

"And now, I have an easier schedule. I only go to the big shows and I can earn a lot that way. But I'm so close to my goal, just really one more season of riding and I can retire from riding to work on my next ideas. I don't have time for a woman, or really the energy to focus on that right now."

"But Emery . . ."

Nash tapped the steering wheel with his thumbs. "Emery is different."

"She's not the girlfriend type?"

"No, not that. I mean, I don't know. She might not be. But she's different because she's always there too. We go to the same shows. We see each other all the time. I like being with her but I don't have to make a real effort to do so." He turned down the radio. "And she's mad as heck most of the time we're together."

"She's really not an angry sort of person."

"I know. I bring out that side of her. I'm not proud of it. And it's basically why I know we'll never be together."

Lacey didn't say anything for a few minutes. "Then why are we going to Tap N' Grill?"

"I don't know, okay? I really don't know. I think I just can't stay away. I can't stand the thought of that creep Isaiah taking advantage of her. I want her to know she has other options, or at least someone on her side."

Lacey nodded, saying nothing.

"Well?" he asked.

"Well, what?"

"Did that answer your question?"

"Sort of. How come you haven't just told her how you feel and given it a try? I mean, if you've been together for so many months already?"

"She's never really given me an opportunity, I guess." He thought about it a moment more. "Or maybe there have been a few times I could have said something but I chickened out. I'm telling you—typically, we don't get along."

"Except you're the one she wanted to take care of me?"

"Yeah." Nash shrugged. "It was a rare demonstration of trust."

"Maybe she thought you'd be the guy I didn't fall for?"

He shifted in his seat. "Why wouldn't you fall for me?"

Lacey laughed. "Does that insult your handsome sensibilities? It's not that. You're hot. But she would trust you to respect the sister relationship or something?"

"There's something to that, an odd sort of trust anyway. For the guy you can't stand to be around but trust with your only family member." He pulled into a crowded parking lot. "Makes an odd sort of sense, I think."

He jogged around to grab Lacey's door, but she opened it herself. "I got this."

He tipped his hat. "You ready for some great cheese fries? These guys make the best queso in the world too."

"I'm here for the dancing too." She linked her arm with his and walked along at his side, practically skipping or bouncing. The woman had more energy than anyone on earth had a right to have. "And the spying."

He laughed. "This better not get back to your sister."

"Not from me, it won't. As far as I'm concerned, we came because Eric gave us the recommendation and then said he'd meet me here."

Nash whistled. "Oh, you're good."

"I have a particular skill."

"Should I be afraid of this skill?"

"Not as long as you're on my side of things."

He held open the door to the Tap N' Grill, and a waft of delicious smelling barbeque drifted out to them. "Now that just reminded me, I'm starving. I hope you want some dinner?"

"Sure thing! I'm game for whatever you are, cowboy."

"That's what Emery calls me sometimes. It's so funny. She's surrounded by men in hats and boots who ride horses and rope cows, but I'm the cowboy."

"It's the highest form of compliment as far as we're concerned."

He reconsidered all the times she'd used that nickname and decided he'd pay closer attention in the future to see if she was trying to compliment him or not.

Loud music, laughter, and good food smells all combined to put Nash in a much better mood. Which was swiftly destroyed the minute the dance floor came into view.

Isaiah was out there with Emery and a whole floor full of dancers. They were spinning and two-stepping and laughing.

Emery's natural happiness was so apparent in the way she carried herself, and in her brilliant smile, that Nash turned around and headed for the door.

Lacey had to tug on his arm. "Wait, where are you going?"

"I can't be here. I'm going to ruin her night."

"What do you mean?"

"She looks so happy in there. Maybe she and Isaiah can get together."

Lacey shook her head.

"What?"

"You are ridiculous. Do you really, in your heart of hearts, think that Isaiah has what it takes to make Emery happy?"

He wanted to say yes just to prove his insecure point, but he couldn't. "No, he doesn't."

"So we're staying. Come on. Pretend you don't see them."

"How could we miss them?"

"That doesn't matter. Let's get a table."

They did and ordered food. Their drinks came. And Emery and Isaiah were still out there dancing.

Nash turned away as much as he could. It might have ruined his whole night, but Lacey was making him laugh, and pretty soon, with a full belly and plenty to laugh about, he was almost in a pleasant enough mood that he could speak civilly to Isaiah, almost.

CHAPTER 10

*E*mery saw Lacey and Nash the minute they stepped into the Tap N' Grill. And she wanted to send them both back out. But this was a free world, and anyone could come to the Tap N' Grill if they wanted. So she ignored them, and brightened her smiles and lengthened her laughs so that maybe they would think she was having so much fun, they could leave her alone.

The music slowed down, and Isaiah pulled her close. "Just in time. I've been wanting to hold you like this all night."

"This is nice."

He rocked her back and forth, one hand cradled in his, the other at the small of her back. "I've never danced with a world-record holder before."

She laughed.

He spun her. And really, he was everything charming. Why couldn't she like this man?

She knew why. It was because of one man who was sitting only twenty feet away and watching them with intense blue eyes from underneath his cowboy hat. He was the real deal. Every inch of him a hardworking, honest cowboy from a generations-old cowboy family. He was her dream. And he was always around. Right now, laughing with her sister.

Even though she was in the arms of a charming, successful man who never made her angry and instead made her laugh, all she wanted to do was to join the table with what felt like her family.

Isaiah looked back over his shoulder at the very table in question. Dang it, her awareness had not gone unnoticed. "Is that Lacey?"

"Yes, I've not seen her this happy in a long time."

"That's good news, isn't it? And maybe with the sponsorship money, you can keep her close and start a life for the two of you here?"

She nodded. "Yes, I'm hoping for that. Maybe even buy a new home. Settle down some day."

He straightened. "But not for a while, right? The contract will go over this, but we're looking for riders who can commit to some time in arenas, traveling to rodeos, winning." Did she imagine it, or did he put an emphasis on the word winning?

"Of course. I'm not ready to retire or anything."

He nodded. "Excellent. One of the many reasons we chose you." He held her closer and lifted the corner of his mouth. "It also helps that you're hot. The cameras will love that, and they already single you out . . ." He raised one eyebrow as if he thought he was flattering her.

"Uh . . ." She spun out and back in. That didn't feel like something she would say thank you for, or appreciate.

"Nash seems to be enjoying your sister. That's great, since he really is a grumpy sort of man lately."

She didn't answer. Nor did she want to gossip about another, especially when Nash had taken time out of his evening to bring her sister to Tap N' Grill. "I'm just happy Lacey seems happy." She spun again and then returned to Isaiah. Time to change the subject. "This is an awesome celebration of a fun milestone, thank you."

"You deserve it. Dinner is on the sponsor. I let them know immediately, and they were overly thrilled with your success. They only wish we could have gotten you some gear or swag to wear during the announcement." He shook his head. "And that's on me. I definitely should speed up the signing and could have easily had a shirt or socks or bandana, or even something to drape across Stargazer while you were beating the world record." He shook his head. "I mean, that's an incredible accomplishment."

"Thank you. It's kind of surreal." She would have said more, but Dakota showed up at Nash and Lacey's table, and they invited her to sit down with them. And then Emery tried not to notice Dakota laughing and leaning across Nash.

Isaiah started telling her something about his childhood and something about how he'd pretended to ride bulls and then went on to setting up his own barrels. She nodded and laughed at what she thought were appropriate places, all the while trying to read the conversation between Lacey, Nash, and Dakota. They seemed to be teasing Nash, who was actually literally blushing, and then Lacey was doing most of the talking. To Emery, she seemed to be planning. Dakota drank and watched with great amusement for most of Lacey's speech, and then Nash acted as though he were drawing on the table with his finger. The other two leaned in closer to see.

Emery couldn't fathom what was being said or even the

topic of conversation. Only one thing was clear. She'd never had a conversation like that with Nash. And watching him tease and laugh and have fun made her realize she was missing a whole side to this man she'd never seen. Suddenly, all kinds of priorities she thought were important faded away in light of a brand new goal. That. Right there.

Isaiah had gone quiet, and she realized she'd not heard a word he'd said for the last bit. She searched his face, which had gone closed and distant.

"Oh no, I've offended you," she said.

"If what I have to say is so uninteresting, maybe we should just go home."

"It's not that at all. I'm distracted by my sister being here. I was watching Dakota, too, and seeing them all laugh together made me happy." She shrugged. "My mind started wandering, and I realized it's been far too long since I laughed very much at all." She widened her eyes, hoping she hadn't just offended the head of her new sponsor.

And that hope right there told her all she needed to know about her feelings for Isaiah. The song ended, and a new, crazy one started back up, but Isaiah seemed deflated. "Let's get a drink." He tugged her hand toward their table.

She was being so unfair to a decent enough man who was her date. She tugged him back. "Wait, first I want to have a little fun too." She waved her hand and started dancing to the faster music.

He glanced over his shoulder at Nash's table, and then he grinned. "Okay." He reached for her hand. "Do you swing much?"

"All the time."

"And lifts?"

"Oh yeah."

He laughed. "Then let's show off a little bit, shall we?"

"Now you're talking." She took his hands and followed his lead, and she was shocked to realize Isaiah was an awesome dancer. She twirled, she spun, she shimmied. He carried her in his arms, he bounced her on his hips and sent her straight up into the air. She was all over the place. And it was a blast. One thing was for sure: She stopped glancing over at Nash's table and enjoyed the date she was on. But she couldn't help but wonder if he saw, and she hoped he wanted to be with her because of it.

Two more dance numbers just like it, and Emery needed a drink and a chair. Out of breath, she pointed to their seats.

Isaiah nodded. When they were seated, he shouted near her ear, "It's so loud in here."

"It really is!" She guzzled her water down. Then she slipped out to go to the bathroom. On her way in, she glanced again toward Nash. No one was at the table. She scanned the crowd. Lacey was with Eric. Emery smiled, and then groaned. Nash and Dakota were in each other's arms, dancing.

She splashed water on her red and sweaty face and cleaned herself up. This night might be the end of her happiness. She shook her head at her own drama. But Nash and Dakota looked more cozy every time she turned around, and she didn't know if she could handle it.

It was time to go home. But then she'd just sit around in her trailer, torturing herself with thoughts of Nash and Dakota. Something had to change. Either she and Nash were going to date, or she was going to get over him. She'd prefer the latter, since dating Nash promised to be complicated.

When she returned to her table, Isaiah had ordered chips and guac and a round of drinks. She studied the tequila, knowing she was not in a good place to be drinking. Over-turned cups told her he'd already downed three, and the effects were kicking in. "Come on. We're just starting this party," he said, downing another.

She lifted her gaze. Nash was watching her with a question in his eyes. She tilted her head toward them, indicating he should join. What was she even doing? But she'd had enough of Isaiah, and drunk Isaiah would be worse.

In less than twenty seconds, Nash, Lacey, and Dakota were crowding into their table. "Oooh, tequila!" Lacey slid the cup over, not drinking. Emery grinned in relief. The last thing she needed was a drunk sister. But then concessions guy showed up and waved her onto the dance floor. She squealed and ran back to him.

Emery shrugged. "I think that might be the last we see of her."

Nash stretched back his arms. He sat next to Emery, and for a minute, she thought he was going to put his arm around her. But when he lowered it, he reached for her hand, gave it a quick squeeze, and then let go.

But she followed his hand and laced her fingers in his. He responded immediately, and then his eyes narrowed at Isaiah.

She shook her head.

Isaiah still sat across from her, with Dakota at his side. "So this is cozy." He downed another.

Emery widened her eyes.

Dakota looked from one to the other and then picked up a glass, lifting it to Emery. "Are you going to drink this?"

"No, it's all yours."

She drank it down. "Thanks. Hey, Isaiah, let's dance." She winked at Nash.

"I'm here with Emery. You don't mind, do you?" He swayed a little bit in his seat, trying to focus on Emery.

"Not at all. Go have fun."

As soon as they left, Emery turned to Nash. "Thank you."

He squeezed their hands and then held them up. "And this means?"

Her face heated immediately, but she held his gaze. "It means everything. Thank you, I need some help, I like you. I want to hold your hand." *Let's make out. Never leave me.* She choked on her thoughts and downed some more water.

She tried to pull her hand back. "I'm sorry. It's silly, but when you pulled your hand away, I didn't want you to." She shrugged.

He tugged her back. "No, I like this. It's new. And . . . makes me want to do a few more things." He wiggled his eyebrows in the most ridiculous way, and she had to laugh.

"Things? Like ranch chores?"

"No, things like . . ." He leaned forward and tucked a strand of hair from her face. "Dance with you."

Her heart leapt forward. "Then let's dance." She tried to scoot toward him and nudge him out of the booth.

But he shook his head. "I'm not dancing with you while you're with Isaiah."

They both turned. He and Dakota were dancing close, really close. And things might even be heating up.

"He's drunk." She shrugged and pointed. "And looking friendly with Dakota."

Nash's mouth twitched into a grin. "Sounds like I'm witnessing two very good reasons to get you out on that floor."

The music switched to something slow, and Dakota melted into Isaiah's arms.

Emery shook her head. "Should I be bugged by that?"

Nash searched her face closely. "Are you?"

She shook her head slowly. "Not in the least."

"Then let's dance."

They stood and walked to the opposite side of the floor, and then Nash pulled her into his arms. They were close, but not touching. His one hand cradled hers like it was special. His other spread along the small of her back, gentle. They swayed a moment, and then he started adding additional steps. When she followed, he added more. Soon, they were making their own little show in the corner of the dance floor. It was slow, smooth, and oh so romantic. Whenever she left his arms for a turn or dip outward, she longed to be back. And they were closer each time.

Their faces were magnetized. So close, she could have drowned in his eyes. The stubble on his chin almost rubbed against her cheek. He smelled of soap and clean clothes and the tiniest bit like a horse. All the better. She smiled.

"I think I've made you smile three times today. That's like a record," Nash said.

And then she laughed.

"Score." He smiled in return, rocking them in place, watching her every expression so closely, it felt like a caress.

"I like it when we're being nice to each other."

"Not just nice. This is all kinds of awesome." He let his fingers spread out further on her back for a moment.

"Can we be like this every day?" She wanted to bite back the words, swallow them away in shy embarrassment.

But he didn't run and hide like she'd always thought he would if she showed the slightest bit of interest. He tilted his head. "We could give it a try . . . You know, we've been at all the same rodeos for the last twenty-four months."

"You noticed? I didn't think you were paying attention."

"Oh, I'm always paying attention."

This was a whole new side of Nash she would like to see a whole lot more of. "Then yes, I did know we've been at all the same shows."

"You've been after the prize money."

She nodded. "I really need it. I'm all me and Lacey have. If I can just save up enough, I've got my eyes on this property." She turned away. "Sorry, you don't need to hear all this."

"No, I want to hear it. That sounds amazing. Where is it?"

"Well, this is the awkward part. It's up by the Dawson Ranch. Up on the other side of the ridge."

He stopped dancing. "You're looking to buy land in Willow Creek?"

She couldn't tell if he was pleased or not, just blank and shocked.

"Um, yes?" She stepped back. "That is, if I can earn the money. I'm almost there. But I think it would be good for us to have a place. The only home we've ever known is the traveling-rodeo kind. And that's just not good for anyone really. Maybe we can settle there. Raise families someday." Her voice caught in her throat. "But Isaiah says he's not looking to sponsor someone who's ready to retire, so sounds like I'll have to put in some time no matter what. But Lacey could move there, get started or something." She looked away. "And now I'm rambling on about it. And you probably think it's weird that I'm moving close to your family after doing every rodeo with you all year . . . stalker much?" She felt her face heat to fever levels. It was time to go.

Nash still hadn't said anything. She stepped farther away and then turned around. Her pace picked up. She could go to the bathroom. Or maybe outside in the cool air. Anything to calm the fire inside.

Of course it was weird to tell Nash she was following him to his home. Which she wasn't. But it was one of the best places to buy land right then. It was beautiful, and one of the few ranching and farming communities that was still thriving. Texas hill country? Yes please. She picked up her pace, not daring to look back.

But then a hand stopped her. Nash. He touched her shoulder and then slid down her arm to her palm, lacing his fingers in his. He was gentle. He was there.

"Do you want to get some air? Go somewhere quiet?" he asked.

She nodded. They both headed for the front door.

A voice called from the dance floor, "Oh. I see how it is! Whoring it with the bull rider now, are you?" Isaiah swayed on his feet, dangerously close to falling.

Dakota whipped around to face him. "What did you just say?" She shoved him with two hands on his chest, and that was all it took for him to fall to the ground.

Half the room broke out into cheers, so her angry frown turned to a cheeky smile and she bowed and waved. Then a tall guy with curly blond hair stepped closer.

She waved to Emery and Nash and then started dancing with him.

Lacey was still distracted by her concessions guy. But she waved them out as well.

"Looks like we have permission to leave." Nash snorted.

"Yes." Emery stared at Isaiah until she saw him sit up. "Let's go."

"Absolutely. I know a place we can talk."

They walked with Nash's hand at her back. He opened

the door to his truck for her and then patted the seat at his side. "This is your seat from now on."

She laughed. "Did you like that? I couldn't tell."

"I did. I'd never let on, of course. But you can't sit anywhere else now."

She scooched over as close as she dared to him.

"Let's get your seat belt on." He grinned and then reached across her body to click her in. "There you go."

She laughed. "Thank you."

He tugged on her hand again, as if it had been too long unattached. All she could do was smile about her situation. She had no idea what would happen with the new sponsor now that she'd left Isaiah drunk and sitting on the floor at Tap N' Grille, but somehow, even so, things were looking up.

CHAPTER 11

*N*ash was going to tread very, very carefully and not somehow ruin whatever this was. Emery sat close. She enjoyed his company. She'd willingly held his hand. And now they were going for a drive. He was still really shocked more than anything that she was buying land in Willow Creek. Shocked and a bit nervous, almost . . . skittish. He laughed at himself. Like a young foal. But suddenly, the idea of Emery not only finally giving him some positive attention, but moving in? That felt like too much, too fast.

He just needed to remind himself that she wasn't doing it for him. She'd be smart to grab any property she could up there. Once the huge ranches had started to create smaller sections for sale, the real estate had jumped through the roof. It was rare. It was excellent. And it had huge potential investment value.

He knew. They'd had to sell off some of theirs.

Did his mother know about Emery's plans? He was still confused about why his mother was calling Emery Banks.

Nothing was making too much sense. His mind sped

through the last few hours. Dakota. Was she fielding inter-ference for him?

Was everyone in the world combining forces to influence and manipulate his life?

Suddenly, his truck felt restrictive. His shirt felt tight. And Emery so close felt . . . a bit claustrophobic. No. No. No. He couldn't ruin this moment with his own need for inde-pendence. No. He raised an arm and pulled her closer. "So talk to me some more about these plans. I don't know what to say. I think it's amazing."

"Oh, stop. I know you're over there cringing and feeling all restricted. You think I'm in your space." She wiggled free, and he lifted his arm.

"Fair."

"Wait, you really are?"

"Didn't you just say . . .?"

"I was testing you. Oh gosh. I really am in your space." She unbuckled. "First, let me move back over here." She slid to the opposite door. "That's better. You can breathe."

And now Nash had gone and ruined everything. "That was a trick question."

"Of course it was. But I wanted to know how you really feel, and now I do. Fair. But Nash, you can't stop a person from buying land near you. It's the best land in the world. It's my dream. And not you or Isaiah or anyone else is gonna take it from me." The tears came quickly, and she turned from him. "Take me home."

"Okay." His voice sounded quiet to him. "Can we make one quick stop first?"

She shrugged, and he took that as a yes.

They drove in silence for a few miles, his mind going

through idea after idea like a NASCAR race. But just like the race, every thought flew by in a blur.

But he pressed on anyway. From what he could gather, he had one chance to turn things around. He turned the truck up the small, steep road that would take them to the ridge.

"You're taking me to Make-Out Point?" Emery's eyebrows raised higher than he'd ever seen them.

"No. I'm taking you to the other side, which is called Have a Heart-To-Heart Talk Point." He had to keep his eye on the narrow road, so he wasn't sure how she took his response. But silence was good with her, maybe. At least she wasn't demanding that he turn around, because that would be dangerous on their current road.

They reached the top. He pulled past a few cars that were, in fact, quite possibly taking advantage of Make-Out Point and pulled around to the opposite side. "It's got the best view of the stars over here."

Nash reached behind them for the thick blankets, and then jogged to her door. "Come on. It's beautiful. And it helps you think." He held up the blankets. "We each get our own?"

Then Emery laughed, and he knew he was in the clear for at least a few minutes. Sheesh. It didn't take much for the two of them to blow up. Was it even a good idea to be with this woman?

They climbed up in the back of his truck, and he thanked the sky for a clear night. The city stretched out in front of them, what there was to see, but the sky stretched above them, and it was filled with stars.

"Oh my." She tipped her head back. "This is really something."

He smiled. "Willow Creek is better, but on a clear night,

this gives quite a show." He laid his blanket down. "Come on, sit against the back with me."

She did, and he was pleased to see she sat close.

"There's your Orion." He pointed to the belt. "It's the first one I find in any sky."

"It's always right there in front of me. Even if I'm not looking. Even from a bedroom window. I always see it." She smiled. "When I was a kid, I thought it was following me around, looking out for me, you know?"

"Someone was. You really are remarkable."

"Our parents abused us."

He swallowed back his surprise at such an admission. He had guessed they weren't the greatest parents. But this was quite a statement.

Emery stared ahead, as if not really seeing anything around them. "We used to hide. If they didn't notice us, they left us alone." Her voice was tight, her breath shaky. "When they died, I was glad for a long time." She looked away. "That sounds so terrible. I felt so guilty for being glad." She held up her hands. "But everything was so much easier. We could find food and hide out at the rodeo. Nothing seemed too terrible when you stopped worrying about being beat up."

Nash just listened. He didn't know what to say. He'd been blessed with his fair share of problems, but nothing like what she had been through. He wanted to hold her hand again but didn't dare. He wanted to act like a boyfriend, but that seemed out of the question. So he just listened. "I'm sorry."

She nodded. "I know it's a huge announcement. I haven't really told anyone else except Billy."

"The more I know about Billy, the more I have to respect that man."

"He's been like a father sort of, maybe an uncle. He never

showed any real physical affection, but I'm happy about that. He just sort of made sure we had what we needed." She snorted. "But he gave us tons to do, that's for sure. Looking back, that's what saved us too. A purpose, respect, lots of work to do, and a safe place to sleep." She nodded. "He's a good man."

"Amen to that. It's the Dawson way. I resented it as a child. But now I'm glad. Rodeo is a lot of work."

"Every single day." Emery sighed and all at once looked really tired.

"Do you wish you could retire?"

She toyed with the fabric on her shirt for a minute. "I love barrel racing. I do. It's such a thrill. I love Stargazer too. And it's been everything for me since I was around twelve years old. But I know I can't do it forever. This seems like a weird time to be talking about it. I just broke the world record. I'm getting a sponsorship, I think. But I don't want to keep going and watch my times dwindle." She laughed. "I guess I'm vain enough to want to step away while I'm still at the top."

"Well, you need a few more shows in you. Nationals will help. Then it puts you solidly there, at the top."

She laughed. "I don't know if I should be offended that you're trying to contest my world record."

He held up his hands. "Who am I to stand between a woman and her world record?"

She shook her head. "I know what you mean. And I need those prizes anyway. I can't step away for at least another six months. And then I think I can do it. Buy the land. Some stock. And see what we make of ourselves."

Nash nodded, to himself mostly. Such an interesting development. Were he and Emery interested in the same darn things in the same darn town? He should be happy about this. He was. But he was feeling that rope tighten, and maybe he was more like the bulls than he cared to admit. He bucked a little at the first sign of any ropes. He knew it. His whole family knew it. Maybe that was why they always seemed to give him his space. Well, he remembered mama's oft-repeated phrase just for him. *I know you'll make the right decision. Give it some thought and prayer.*

He laughed to himself. Then he pointed up to the North Star. "Everyone always talks about that star guiding people, leading the sailors where they need to go and all that."

Emery nodded. "That's because it does guide people. You know it's true north . . ."

"Yes, I know. Hear me out. I'm all about that. But what if you don't want to go where everyone else is going just because they want to be in the north? What if you want to go west? Or even south?"

"Then you go, but that star, it still guides you because you put it behind you."

"Yes. Exactly. So no matter what I've wanted to do my whole life, be a Dawson, separate from the Dawsons, find a new branch of Dawson, it's always with that one star in mind, the Dawson star. It's been guiding me no matter what I do."

She nodded.

"What's your north star? I think once you figure it out, you'll have all your answers."

She looked pretty sure of herself. And he was touched by her surety. "You already know," he said.

Emery nodded. "But it's personal, and maybe something you don't want to talk about right now."

"I'm all about listening. Already, I've learned that I need to do a lot more of that."

"I've just always tried to put Jesus there." She held up her hands. "I know. That's what a lot of people say, but it doesn't make it any less true for me. He's gotten me out of a lot of scrapes, and I've never gone wrong following Him along."

"That's something my mama would say. And I agree with you. But I don't know. Is He really that aware of all the small stuff? How can we even know what He thinks about it all?"

"I don't always know. But I believe He's guiding me and helping me make my dreams come true. I believe in gut feelings and I believe in working to make things happen, knowing He will back me up and help me find my way. If good things happen, I thank Him. Glory to Him. If hard things happen, I know He's holding me up. It's kind of like, whatever my life becomes will be beautifully made because of Him."

"And if you mess it all up?"

"If I make a mistake, He takes care of that too. I think He expects me to get things wrong sometimes."

Nash felt like he did on the very best Sundays in church, when the person speaking up in front really reached him, except he could ask questions, and he had one.

"But your life. It's been tough."

Emery searched his face a minute. "Do you mean, you're not sure how beautifully made it's been so far?" She nodded. "Yeah, that's true. And I didn't have any choice in the parents I got. But a long time ago, I learned it doesn't do a bit of good to be angry. And blame certainly doesn't help anything." She sighed. "And our lives just hardly ever go the way we planned. And I have to have faith that if God's helping me, I'd rather have things go His way, you know? That's tough when you want something real bad, like achingly, crazily, desperately want something. You have to ask, are you willing to let it go?"

Nash was kind of in awe of this woman in the back of his truck. Suddenly, he wanted to hold her hand, but it wasn't for all of the same reasons as before. He wanted to be at her side. He wanted to help her reach her dreams. He wanted her in his life.

And that thought about nearly choked all other reasonable thoughts from him.

"See, I knew you'd be uncomfortable. Sorry. You did ask, though."

"No, not at all." He shook his head too many times. "I'm perfectly comfortable talking about Jesus. Just ask my mama." He laughed. "But I think what I'm feeling right now is a bit . . . intimidated?" He shrugged. "You've been doing so good with the trust and the faith. Sometimes, I forget." He considered what they'd talked about at the last Sunday dinner he'd zoomed in for. "But I really do believe God is aware of the details, and He loves us. Two things that help me when I give it thought."

"When He's all you have, you never forget." Her words were made even more true by the life she had lived to back them up.

This time, Nash wrapped his arm around her shoulders, trying to take some of that burden. "I'm sorry." He didn't want to be sorry she'd had to rely on Jesus. She loved Him and she understood Him a heck of a lot better than Nash did. But he was sorry that life was hard. He just was.

She rested her head on his shoulder for a moment. "That saying is true, how God helps us with other people? I've always felt that."

He leaned his head back, enjoying the feel of her warm body next to him in the chilly night air. "Billy."

"Yes, Billy, Lacey, and you." The last addition of him was spoken so quietly, so tentatively, he wasn't sure she really said it. But he took it anyway. And he was humbled. She viewed his ornery, rough, argumentative presence in her life as a gift from God? He'd better up his game.

"Sorry I make things harder than they need to be."

She laughed. "Kettle. Pot. Come on. I'm as difficult as they come. And I can't promise I won't be difficult again tomorrow."

"I would expect nothing less." He lifted her hand in his and then brought it to his lips. "But can we have moments like this too, in between, so I know you like me."

"I never said anything about liking you." She wiggled against his side.

"Oh yes, you did. I remember very clearly you telling me you held my hand because you liked me."

She opened her mouth and then closed it again. "You're right. And it's true, I do like you. I can't explain it, but I like you a lot." She laughed.

The sight of her eyes sparkling in the moonlight, her hair falling all around her, was maybe the most beautiful thing he'd ever seen.

"Well, good, because I like you too."

Emery stopped. "You do?"

"I . . . do." He realized the implications of those two words. And wasn't even bothered by it. "I've liked you for a long time, Emery Banks. I just didn't know what to do about it."

She sat forward so that their faces were close. "And now?"

Nash shook his head. "I still have no idea."

She laughed and looked away.

He missed her closeness. Before he could think better, he brought her back with a finger on her chin. He stared long enough into her eyes that she would know he was sincere. "Except for this." He closed the distance and pressed his lips to hers. Once, softly, though stopping there was killing him. Her lips were open and velvety. And tasted of strawberries even though she'd been dancing all night. "Mm." He smiled. "That's what I've also been wanting to do for a long time."

"What if I told you that wasn't near enough?"

He grinned. "Then you'd have one happy cowboy on your hands."

"Well, come on, then. That wasn't near enough." Her eyes dared him. Her mouth quirked up in a sexy smile, and he knew he was a goner. She shifted so she could lean an arm across his upper body.

He sat forward, running fingers through her hair a moment. She closed her eyes and tipped her head back. Miles of gorgeous neck and creamy skin invited his mouth to explore. But he wrapped an arm around her back, tugging her closer, and brushed his lips softly against hers. "Something like this?"

Emery shook her head.

"Oh? Maybe a bit more, then?"

She nodded.

With one stroke more, his upper lip sliding along her lower, he tempted himself with her goodness. "Mm. I like that."

She looked like she might bite his mouth next time he tried to lengthen this out any more. He loved that fire in her eyes. Who knew that all the feistiness he saw in her every day had its benefits? She closed her eyes, and then he captured her mouth with his.

And there was nothing but good in that kiss. He was hungry for more. She responded to everything he did, every shift in pressure, every pause, everything.

If this was how kisses were with Emery, he was just going to spend the rest of his life kissing her. She leaned into him, and he dipped her slowly in his lap, tenderly teaching her just how much he was enjoying her kiss, until he knew things were too good and he needed to take a break. With a reluctance that was like nothing else he'd ever experienced, he slowed things down and created some distance, which she fought at first.

"Woman." He growled.

And then she laughed. "What?"

"Come now. We're supposed to be looking at the stars." He still held her in his arms, her brilliant eyes looking up at him with such amusement and caring, he could hardly stop himself from kissing her all over again. But he did. He lifted her back up but kept her close. "Thanks for coming up here with me."

She leaned back against his shoulder, his arm around her. "You're welcome."

They sat together, talking mostly about nothing. He toyed with her fingers and kissed her head through her hair now and then. It was the most comfortable, desire-filled evening Nash had ever had.

CHAPTER 12

Do not fear. I am with you. Be not dismayed. For I am your God and will give you aid. How simple and powerful those words are on the page. And how difficult to implement at times. At other times, I am filled with peace. I much prefer the peace. And still, there is something exciting about the unknown. Even though it invites worry, it is also a beautiful opportunity. Nash kissed me.

The next morning, Emery woke with a smile, and then gasped and frowned. "What am I gonna do?"

Lacey poked her head through the divider and into Emery's bedroom. "Just remembered you kissed Nash?" She laughed like she was the most hilarious person in the world.

"No. I just remembered I left Isaiah on the floor, drunk, last night."

Lacey waved her hand. "Oh that? I wouldn't worry one minute about that. He had Dakota all over him the rest of that night. He was just fine."

Some alarm bells rang at the sound of Dakota maybe

milking him for some of that sponsorship money. Emery groaned. "We're supposed to meet today to sign contracts."

"I guess now we'll see what he's made of."

"I guess so." She rolled over and put a pillow on her head.

"And Nash?" Lacey landed down on her bed beside her with a flourish. "Do tell."

"I'm in so much trouble. If that man isn't serious about me, I'm gonna lose it all over again, because I don't think I can ever love another after a kiss like that."

Lacey squealed and shouted, "Emery and Nash sitting in a tree."

"Actually, it was the back of a pickup," Nash called from outside.

Both sisters gasped.

"And Isaiah's pulling up." His voice came from just outside the door.

"Thank you." Emery leapt out of bed. "I gotta hurry and get ready."

"I bet you look smoking hot first thing in the morning. Can I come in?" Nash asked.

"No!" both women called back.

Emery threw a clean shirt over her head. "Stall Isaiah."

"Worst job ever," he called in. "But I'm on it."

Emery brushed her teeth, trying to talk at the same time. "What am I gonna say to Isaiah?"

"I guess it depends what he says to you," Lacey replied. "But he said the committee or the board or whoever already picked you. He'd be a real obvious creep if he broke the deal now just because of last night."

"No one said he's not a potential creep. That could be our reality."

"Well then, so? What happens if you don't get the sponsorship? You've been doing amazing without it. You have the world record. There's gotta be someone else who wants to pick you up."

Lacey had a point. But it was still uncomfortable. And her first choice was Bunson, even if she had to deal with Isaiah. "Should I feel bad? We were on a date."

"No. Seriously, Em. He probably hooked up with Dakota from the looks of things."

"I didn't think she was like that."

"Well, me either, but I can't wipe away what I saw with my own eyes. And it was not exactly appealing either."

Emery laughed. "He's hot, people say."

"Oh, he is. But once you suspect him of using his position to get women, it just goes downhill from there. His nose started to bother me."

"It bothered me too. It turns up a little bit at the end. Like you would expect a girl's to." Emery laughed again and then shook her head. "Listen to me. I sound kind of shallow."

The sound of men approaching, with Nash speaking overly loud, made Emery smile. "Okay. How do I look?"

"Like you just got out of bed." Lacey threw her a brush.

"Oh, bother with the hair. Brush." But she ran it through her hair until the long strands shimmered. Then she added a little extra mascara to what she hadn't washed off last night. "That's gonna have to do."

"I approve. Now, where do you want me?"

"Oh, right. Don't leave me."

"I can't be in the meeting with you."

"Go back into your room." She smiled. "Otherwise, it's a guy in here with me by myself. That's awkward enough. And kind of creepy 'cause it's him."

"Did you ever stop to consider he might be a perfectly normal guy and we're blowing this out of proportion?"

"Of course. I was dating him, remember, up until last night?"

"When he really did start to act a little off."

"True."

Nash laughed overly loudly. "Too true, man. Hey, I think the girls are in there. At least I don't think anyone has left yet."

"Thanks. Let's talk some more about your ideas. I think the board would be intrigued by half of them at least. All for a buck or two, right?"

"Yeah, or a lot more."

"Right, okay, thanks, man." Isaiah knocked.

Lacey leapt for her room and slid the door shut.

Emery exhaled and then opened the door. "Oh hey, Isaiah." She smiled, going for apologetic.

But he beat her to it. "I'm afraid I'm going to have to apologize." He shook his head.

"Oh hey, don't worry about it. Everyone gets drunk now and then."

He tilted his head, "Oh no, not that. I wasn't exactly drunk."

"Oh, right." She hid her smile. "All right, then. Well, do you want to come in?"

He shook his head. "No, this won't take long. I just came by to tell you that the board is reconsidering an additional sponsor at this time."

Emery raised a hand to her chest. "Reconsidering sponsoring me?"

He nodded, looking into her face like he was telling her about the weather.

"What are you talking about? You said they approved me."

"Well, they did, but they're fickle, and with additional information, they felt that in today's unstable rodeo market, perhaps they should hold off on bringing on an additional sponsorship."

Emery narrowed her eyes and put her hands on her hips. "What additional information?"

His smile was slow and lazy. "I'm not aware of all their in-house discussions, but I believe it had something to do with loose morals."

She nearly choked. "Pardon me?" Standing taller, nearly spitting out her next words, she tried to sound at least partly professional. "As if my personal life is any of their business. And speaking of my personal life, I do not have loose morals. I don't even drink, like some other people I know. And again, what business is it of theirs anyway?"

"They make it very much their business. You would be a face on their brand, a public personality. Any bad press surrounding you would be a reflection on them, and they felt that your background, your questionable family situation, those kinds of things were perhaps not the most stable, solid choice."

Emery's throat tightened to the point of making it difficult to breathe, and she gasped in new air. "That is completely unfair. Didn't you tell them that I'm not a risk? That I have a good reputation?"

He shrugged. "I had before. I could have reminded them, but nothing in your bar behavior last night led me to believe anything other than what they were concerned about. I had to agree."

She felt the blood leave her face. "You . . . You let a personal grudge . . . You decided that since we didn't get together last night, that you would withhold your recommendation? What kind of pig are you?"

Isaiah laughed. "Your temper also had something to do with it." He checked his watch. "Name-calling already at eight in the morning." He shook his head. "We'll be looking around for additional options. Perhaps one of your friends will earn the spot. You can at least be happy it stays in the Mesquite family." He lifted a hand in Dakota's direction, but she didn't wave in response.

"Goodness, everyone is in a bit of a temper this morning."

"Isaiah. Come on. Put in a good word for me. You know this isn't right. They're being influenced by false information."

"Do I know that, though?" He headed back in the direction of his car. "Perhaps if we had been able to get to know each other better." He dug his keys out of his pocket and clicked to unlock his car doors. "I'll be at the rodeo tomorrow night. Good luck on your race. I hear you have some stiff competition, and maybe even another contender for that world record of yours." He started whistling and then climbed into his car.

She slammed the door.

"Aaaaah!" Screaming did nothing to help her feel better.

Lacey opened the door. "So that was bad?"

"That was very bad. They withdrew the offer to sponsor me, saying I had a questionable or problematic family background and loose morals."

"What a liar."

"Should I go apologize and make it right with him?"

"What? No way."

"We need that sponsorship money, Lacey. Do you want to live in a trailer at the side of a rodeo for the rest of your life?"

"I thought you liked this life."

"I do. But not forever. Don't you ever want your own life? Land? A home?" Emery felt herself crumbling. "I need . . ." She stepped away from Lacey like she might go to her bed, but that wasn't far enough. She pushed open the door. "I'm going for a ride."

"Uh, okay. Can I do anything?"

Emery waved her off. Her chest was tight, her throat tight, her neck almost unable to rotate, it was so stiff.

Nash lifted a hand in her direction, but she waved him off too.

CHAPTER 13

*N*ash watched Emery storm off toward the barn. She'd be all right. Stargazer would take care of her. Nash had a bone to pick with one Isaiah Thornton. He rotated his shoulders around a few times. Man, he'd like to just punch him in the face like they used to do as kids. Someone bother you? Wrestle them to the ground. In five minutes, everyone would be laughing anyway. But this was not a kid problem and wouldn't be solved any sooner with a facer. The only thing that would help was to get a healthy dose of personal satisfaction. And there was nothing wrong with that, as far as he was concerned. But he wasn't going to go confront Isaiah to help himself.

He swung himself up and into his truck. It was a real shame, what he was about to do. He'd liked having a sponsor —and all the extra gear, that was nice too. And the money was nice. But this guy, someone had to stop him. And some-times that someone was Nash.

Then his phone rang. He slid the call on. "Mav."

"Hey, Nash, how's it going?"

He resisted grunting like a gorilla and tried to find some sense of respectability. He always assumed Mav was checking up on him. That was what older brothers did. "I'm good, man, how's everything at home?"

"Oh, it's great. We miss you, of course. But we're real proud of you, winning all the time. That's some prize money, I bet."

"Yeah, it's great."

"So are you coming back for Willow Creek Days? I heard a rumor about some baby pigs?" Mav would know some of what he was doing with Grace, his daughter.

"Yeah, I'll be there to at least cheer Grace on. I feel like she's got it, though. How are things?"

"Great. I think you're right. She's loving this. I wanted to call and just tell you thanks. It's meant so much to her. She's a new person, with a purpose. I just hope you get to see some of what's happening with these kids."

"Oh yeah?" Nash took a seat. He was suddenly real interested in this conversation.

"Yep. They're doing it all—4-H and training and even showing. Their grades are up. We've even heard they're more respectful at home. The program is raising the next generation."

Nash smiled and nodded. "That's what it's all about, Mav. Right there."

"I gotta admit, you're right, and thanks for making Grace such a huge part of it all."

"What could I do? She named her pig after me."

"That pig is so dang fat. It's a waste of space."

"But she won't let you kill it?"

"Nope. And it's a prize winner too. Blue ribbons three years running."

Nash laughed. "My legacy lives on."

"Don't even talk to me about legacy. Because the dang thing is named Nash, I'm gonna have to look at its glorious snout for the rest of its long, pampered life."

Laughter took some of Nash's frustration away.

"I'm also calling about your head."

Nash rotated his neck, suddenly now wanting an excuse to end the conversation.

"If you need some cash to tide you over, or even another investor or something, the ranch has money for that. We're all working together on things. No one has to do anything all by themselves."

He loved the sound of what his brother was saying, but Nash had spent his whole life living off the others. And at the end of the day, he wanted to feel like he'd contributed to things as well. "I got things covered, bro."

"But if you want out now, even, just want to start your other businesses? You have your portion to invest."

"I know that. I got this, I'm telling you. Just a few more times on a bull and I'm done anyway. It's all going to work out great, and then I'll knock your boots off with what I'm bringing in."

"What are you bringing in?"

"Well, you know about the kids' stuff."

"Yep. We love it. And?"

"Just trust me on this. I want to work it out. Then we can talk."

"Nash, I trust you. Of course. But our brand is a family business. We work together."

"I know. Look, Mav, I gotta run. Don't worry, big brother. This is one thing you can just leave to me."

Nash sensed the reluctance in the long pause before Mav said, "Looking forward to it. Take care of yourself."

"I will, thanks."

He was about to dial Isaiah's number, but he hesitated. What would happen if he ticked off his sponsor and got kicked off? He'd just told Mav he would take care of things. This was not taking care of things. It would sure as heck feel good, though. Isaiah needed to learn a thing or two.

He lowered the phone, then picked it up again. "Billy," he said to himself.

The man answered straightaway. "What can I do for you, Nash?" His deep, low, friendly voice was something Nash would miss if he ever stepped too far away from this world.

"Billy, we have a situation."

The man listened to everything Nash had to say with an occasional grunt or two, and then he took his time before answering.

"Now that's a mighty big pickle our little lady has got herself into."

Nash choked on a laugh but he kept listening.

"The way I see it, there are other sponsors in the world, and she might be better off with one of them."

"That's for sure. But do we just let her walk away and not do anything about it? That's unethical, to say the least."

"We don't have any proof of anything, though, do we? From what I understand, she went to the bar with Isaiah and came home with you." The pause was lengthy.

Nash sighed. "So you're saying I ruined this for her." His shoulders dropped in resignation. What the man said made sense.

"Now listen here, son. I'm not saying you ruined a darn

thing. I think the opposite could be argued in this situation. All I'm saying is that we couldn't be complaining to any board or ethics committee when facts are facts. Everything he's been doing is on the subtle side of things, if you know what I mean."

"Yeah, I know, like a snake in the grass."

Billy's laugh was low and slow, the kind that came from deep in his belly. "Looks to me like she's doing all right for herself. I don't think I'd get my boots all bent about it. You just keep getting yourself healed so we see you up on a bull end of this month."

"Yes, sir."

"And Nash?"

"Yes, sir?"

"Take care of yourself. A good man knows when it's time to step away."

"Hmm. Thank you." He hung up, unsure if Billy was talking about giving Emery her space or quitting the rodeo. And he didn't like the sound of either option. *A good man knows when it's time to step away.* He wasn't stepping away from anything just yet, no matter what anyone spouted in his direction.

His phone rang again. "Mama." Nash smiled. No matter when she called, it was good to talk to his mother.

"I hear you're not resting."

He groaned, thinking maybe sometimes it wasn't always the greatest time to talk to his mother. "I'm resting. I haven't been up on a bull one time since the injury."

"Well, that's good now, you keep it up. And whatever other business or personal things you got going, you take it easy. If you rest, you can get back up on the bulls. If not, you might be resting for a lot longer."

"I know. And I'm taking care. Now, what can I do for you?"

"You know I love that question." He could hear her smile, and it made him grin too.

"Well, ma'am, you raised me right."

"I'm looking forward to this coming weekend. You're still coming?"

"I am."

"And you'll bring that Emery of yours?"

He shook his head. "Not sure why you're calling her mine, but I like the sound of that so I won't be correcting you."

"I knew you would see the light. She's one diamond of a woman, and that Lacey too. She's gonna be just fine."

"Thanks, Mama. I don't know how much she needs me, but I'm glad she's coming to Willow Creek Days. Knowing you would be good for her."

"Oh, you're just not seeing what a catch you are. But I'm loving her no matter what you two decide."

"I know, Ma, thank you."

"Take care of yourself."

"I always do."

"No, son, that's the quick answer. I need you to think real long and hard about this and decide to put your health first."

"Hmm. I promise to think long and hard. But how many bull riders do you know that put their health first?"

"All the ones who are still alive and walking and thinking on their own."

He sighed. "Okay, Mama, I'll be careful." That was all he could promise. And now he really needed to go.

"I'll talk to you later, son. Love you."

"Love you too."

He pocketed his phone, grabbed his chores bag, and stepped out his trailer door. Time to get this day going.

Billy found him on his way to start the chores. "You know, son, I've been thinking some more."

"Glad to hear it." Nash tipped his hat.

"Those girls are real deserving. I'm thinking Dakota is too. And I don't like the idea of Isaiah lingering around trying to take advantage of good people."

"Now, I don't either."

"So I wanted you to know, I'll be watching him, and I'm not afraid of mentioning something, even if it's vague. Then more people are aware, if you know what I mean."

"You've been good to them both. You're a good man, Billy."

He tipped his hat. "Thank you, son. I feel the same way about all you Dawsons. What are your plans when all this is over?"

Nash hadn't told too many folks about his stock idea. But Billy would be a good one. He might even want to hire Nash's stock company sometime.

"I thought I'd start managing stock." He almost winced, waiting to hear from one of the old pros in the business why it was a terrible idea.

But instead, Billy's old, weathered face broke out into a wide grin. "Nash Dawson, that's the smartest idea you've ever had, right after being interested in our Emery. Talk to me, son. What do you have figured out?"

Nash breathed out in relief. He didn't know why telling people his idea was such a frightening moment, but it was probably related to his fear of failing. He just really wanted it to work.

"How close are you to gathering up the capital you need to get started?"

"About four more rides, if I can ever get back on a bull."

"That all? Son, I'll spot you that. You just pay me back when you're on your feet. Oh, and count on the Mesquite Rodeo to use your services when you have enough award-winning stock that I can use 'em."

"Oh, we've got a great bull. He's ready to ride nationally, but we need to keep him close so we can build our lines."

"But you'll breed him."

Nash nodded. "You bet we will."

"Then maybe we can pay to use this bull of yours, get you started."

"That'd be real nice of you, Billy. And he won't let you down. I've ridden him, and I get super high marks every time. Besides, he's a showman himself. I swear he likes to liven things up a little bit."

Billy laughed. "Sometimes I wonder about these animals. I wouldn't be a bit surprised." He paused a moment more and then he cleared his throat. "I've been thinking about your mama."

Nash's mouth tugged up in a grin. "Oh, you have."

"Yes. And I was wondering . . . Well, son, there ain't no easy way to say this, but I'd like to court her, you know, but I want to do it right." He rubbed his face. "I'm not sure how to go about it, and every time I try to let her know, I feel like I'm being a sneaky coward. Should I talk to Maverick?"

Nash had no idea how that conversation would go down. His brother might not take it too kindly out of principle. "Does my mother know?"

"Well now, I'm not sure. I'm trying to let her know, but I

think I might be failing at it. I figure before I do anything too obvious, I should talk to you boys."

He paused, and Nash let him wait a second. Dating his mother was not an easily won privilege, after all. "I think it's certainly up to my mother who she spends time with, and I just don't even know what she would say. I know she has all kinds of respect for you. We all do. And Dad sure liked you. But of all the brothers, Mav is the one you have to convince. You coming out next weekend?"

"Yes I am. I'm still planning on it."

"Then this is going to be one interesting week at home." He thought of the event and the children's events and Emery at home and now Billy. "Of course you'll come for Sunday dinner."

"I've already been invited. And I might stay some extra time at the house too. If that's okay with you."

Nash was surprised but not concerned. "Like I said, Mav is the one you have to talk to."

"Then I bet we can help each other out here. Do I have a deal?"

"Wait a minute, you offering to help me start my stock management if I help put in a good word with Mav?"

"Yep, that's what I'm saying."

His smile grew. "You've got yourself a deal."

"Excellent. Come on by before our trip out there to talk details. I'm serious about being involved. I'd like to see what I can do. I'm already thinking of some good breeding animals you might want to get yourself ahold of."

"Excellent. And I might be able to help you know the way straight to Mama's heart."

"Dishes, flowers, and fixing things around the house?"

Nash raised his eyebrows. "Yep. And some good Bible reading around the table. Brush up on your Psalms."

"That's my favorite part."

"Then you'll do just fine."

When they parted, Nash felt lighter than he had in a long time. Things were most definitely looking up.

Emery's frustrated holler came from the barn, and he was jerked back into her circumstance. Things were most definitely not looking up for her.

He jogged that way, unsure what he would find, and not really knowing how to help her.

CHAPTER 14

*E*mery watched Nash walk away from Billy, looking as pleased as he had in a long time. And then because she was watching him, she ran into the low entrance and fell off her horse.

She landed on her arm and it didn't feel great, a kind of sharp pain she'd never felt before. And when she stood, it didn't hang right. But once she wiggled it a little bit, it seemed fine. Stargazer had taken off into the middle of the arena and was kicking and bucking up into the air. Definitely expressing some thoughts about not being taken out at all over the past couple days. She stood to watch her a moment, holding her arm.

Nash jogged up to her side. "Hey, how you doing?" He bumped her with his shoulder. But the pain that shot through her arm was so acute, she called out, "Oh man. Oh ow." She winced. "No, no, no. This is not happening to me."

"What happened?" He moved his hands forward like he would touch her arm.

"Don't do that." She shook her head. "It's weird. I can

move. See." She opened and closed her hand and lifted and lowered her arm. But when she tried to put it up above her head, she cried out again. "This is not happening."

Carefully, gently, Nash stepped close and kissed her forehead. "I think we should get you into an urgent care to take a look."

Her horse whinnied and kicked up her back legs again. "What's going on out there?" he asked.

"I'm not totally sure, but she's definitely got opinions. She brushed me off under the entrance."

"What?!" He frowned.

"But you know, I usually duck, so I don't blame her, or I didn't until I'm seeing this massive amount of attitude going on." She laughed. "What's gotten into her?"

Stargazer ran by them, kicking up dirt from the arena as she flew around the entire perimeter like she was on a racetrack.

"Would you look at her go? She's fast. Do you know her parentage?"

"Billy would know better. But I think she's got some racehorse in her. Something fancy like that. She's the best, maneuvers well, everything."

"Have you ever thought about breeding her?"

Emery was taken aback and began to shake her head, but then paused. "No, I haven't. I suppose I could, once we're done." She pointed out to the arena. "But look how much she loves to run. I couldn't take that from her."

"I'm not saying take it from her, but she would have some valuable foals, I'm guessing."

Emery studied him. "Something happened. On the phone."

He huffed out a breath. "Lots of things. But one thing

didn't happen. I got on the phone to call out Isaiah. He is so beyond inappropriate and someone needs to tell him. But I had to stop before I dialed."

She breathed out in relief. "Thank heavens."

"Well, hear me out. I don't think there's anything wrong with telling him exactly where he's in the wrong, but I'm not sure I'm the one to do it."

"Billy."

Nash shook his head.

Her eyes widened. "Me?"

"Yes, I think you're the one to do it."

"But I already did, didn't I?"

"You probably did let him know you were unhappy, but if you feel like it, sometime, it would be good to let him know what his position and the awkward place he put you in with your relationship did to you. And you could report him to his board." Nash nodded.

Emery thought long and hard in the few minutes he turned to stare at the horse gifted to her. Maybe he was right. Maybe he was wrong. She was not one to make waves, and why did she need more waves in her life right now? What she needed was smooth sailing out the door. But maybe that just wasn't how life worked.

"Are things ever just . . . blessed?" she asked.

"Sure, what do you mean?"

"I mean, like you show up late and there is a parking spot open just for you, or you forget your paperwork but something reminds you to grab it before you get too far away. Or, you know, you meet the perfect guy and it all falls together just right. Some people have these charmed lives, and I just don't think I'm one of them."

Nash stepped closer. "I think there's plenty of evidence

you're one of them. At least some might look at you and think so anyway."

"Then they don't know what they're talking about."

"Of course not. And you don't, either, when you say some people have these marvelously charmed lives." He stuck his hands in his pockets. "Everybody's got something."

Emery lifted her arm as if it were in a sling and then carried the weight of it with her other hand. "This is starting to throb." She laughed, but there were tears in her eyes. "And you can't tell me that breaking my arm right now doesn't just absolutely suck."

He breathed out a long, slow breath. "I know it does.' He pointed to his head. "Concussion, remember?"

"Oh right. I'm sorry."

"No, that's okay, but let's go see what the doc says. You never know. It might be easier than we think."

She whistled, and Stargazer came running.

"Whoa, now that's a good horse."

"She really is, and it's not going to be fun when I put her back in her stall without even a decent workout."

"Oh hey, I'll ride her."

"Can you? With your head?"

"As long as she doesn't buck me to the ground."

"No guarantees."

Nash laughed. "We'll be just fine. Besides, I have to convince this woman I know to like me."

Emery shook her head. "What does Stargazer have to do with that?"

"Because no good woman worth her salt is going to trust a man her horse doesn't like."

Emery had to hand it to him. He was absolutely correct.

"You know Stargazer doesn't like Isaiah."

They both laughed.

And when Stargazer came running to them, she nuzzled Emery and then sniffed in Nash's direction before running off again.

"Oh boy, she's almost as much work as her owner." Nash chuckled and then walked out into the arena.

"Here." Emery tossed him a carrot. "And I am not work."

"Ah, now she tells me." He caught the carrot and walked out into the arena, making clucking noises.

At first, Stargazer wanted to show off a little bit more, but as soon as she saw the carrot, she made her way over to Nash pretty easily. He pet her and talked quietly, running his hands over her back and down her legs and on her head. "There, are we friends?"

She bobbed her head a couple times, which told Nash that they weren't exactly friends. She was feeling feisty and would like to buck him off if given the chance.

But he didn't have time to set her perfectly at ease. He needed to get Emery to the doctor before her arm started to swell.

He grabbed a handful of her mane and then leaped up onto her bare back.

For a minute, she shifted in place, breathing out with her nose. Her ears seemed interested more than anything, rotating forward and back, and Nash thought that maybe he could get a couple laps in the arena out of her, and she'd be happier to return to her stall.

"There's a girl, Stargazer."

She nickered and trotted over to Emery, as if it didn't matter one whit that someone was on her back and might have other plans.

"Oh boy, she's in a mood," Nash said.

"She really is. Might be a good idea just to slide right off." Emery reached for the reins. "We can bring her back to her stall, and come back later and get her that exercise she needs."

Emery watched Stargazer nervously. She knew exactly what was going through that horse's mind, and it involved Nash on his butt in the dirt. She raised her uninjured hand to the horse's nose. "There now. Come on. It's time to eat your oats. You're gonna love it, and then we'll take you out after the doc." She rested her forehead against her horse's head. "That's my pretty girl."

She nickered and held still for Emery, which she appreciated. The last thing she wanted was for Nash to hurt his head. "Whoa, girl."

"Well look at that, the two lovebirds." Isaiah's voice was grating. Stargazer lifted her head and pawed the ground, apparently nervous about his approach.

"Stargazer. Come on now."

Nash eyed Isaiah but winked at Emery. "You're not worried about me on a horse, are you?"

Isaiah approached, probably the last person in the world she wanted to see right now. She stopped cradling her arm and stood taller. "Isaiah."

"I came looking for you both. How convenient and predictable that I would find you together, though this is interesting. Emery, holding her arm like it hurts. Nash on Stargazer bareback? What am I missing?"

Emery kept one hand on her horse's flank. "What do you want? Come to offer life-changing sponsorships and then take them away? Oh wait, you already did that." She frowned. "I'm really not interested in whatever you have to say."

"You might be, since it involves another sponsorship offer."

She went very still. "What did you say?"

"Turns out the board wasn't very interested in offending Billy Thornton." He arched a brow in Nash's direction. "And they would like to offer you our full sponsorship package, beginning immediately, and they hope you'll represent us in Willow Creek next week." He lifted a chin in Nash's direction. "With this guy here. We're going to do a king and queen of Bunson. Guess what, lovebirds? You're it." He seemed to be enjoying himself, but Emery couldn't really tell. "Of course, that all depends on whether or not you can ride. And we know this guy can't yet."

Nash shifted his weight, still sitting atop Stargazer. "Yes I can. Doc cleared me after four weeks. That's Willow Creek."

He dipped his head. "I stand corrected. And you, Emery? Is there something going on with your arm?"

She shook her head. They had no diagnosis, nothing. It hurt. Arms hurt sometimes.

"Excellent. Then we will see you both there. Check your emails for travel details, instructions on what to wear, and scheduled itinerary for the event. We have box seats in their rodeo arena, but I imagine the Dawsons do as well. You can sit where you like."

"Will you be there?" Now that he was forced to offer her what he'd done in the beginning, and he seemed so unhappy about things, Emery's heart softened a bit toward him.

"I haven't decided."

"And Dakota?"

He stopped walking and went very still. "You know, you women who go after the guy with the brand name just to get ahead are no better than the guy who enjoys the attention."

He dipped his head and picked up his pace. Then he stopped again. "Your contract will also be in the email. Sign it. These things have a way of slipping away."

Emery felt that comment all the way down to her toes, and not in a good way. "Oh, he's right." She brought a hand to her mouth. "Am I a terrible person?"

"I've always thought so." Nash's eyes twinkled down at her. "Come on. You're not a terrible person. He's just unhappy. Sounds like Dakota didn't last either."

"He's a great guy."

"But is he really? I wasn't seeing a lot of great-guy vibe in him."

"I thought so, at least some of the time."

"There, see, you *weren't* just using him to get a sponsor."

"Maybe a little bit. But it wasn't really that. I was flattered. He's a powerful man. I enjoyed the attention." She sighed rubbed Stargazer on the nose. "I didn't really think about it quite like that until you and I started fighting in a nicer way." She laughed. "I thought I was interested, until . . ." She shrugged.

Nash laughed too, lifting his face to the sky. "Fighting in a nicer way? Is that what we were doing?"

Stargazer shifted again. And then somewhere from the parking lot, a car alarm went off. That was enough for her horse. Emery tried to reach for her, but she lifted both front legs in the air, kicked around multiple times, and then turned fully around and raced back out to the arena.

"Stargazer! No!"

But she looked like there was no stopping her until she got whatever this was out of her system. She raced here and there and bucked, full on kicked up her back legs and then her front. And at the same time as Emery worried for Nash, she saw why he'd thought her worry was funny. The man was a national bull-riding champion. And while bulls weren't the same as riding bareback or bronc, he certainly had skills. Which were on full display.

But with every jerk of his head, she winced and grabbed her own with her good arm. They were a pair, both injured, both trying to stay on an animal.

Her horse spun in the air.

Nash had a full handful of her mane and whooped in the process. "What else you got?" he called out.

And Emery could only laugh. Stargazer stilled for a moment. Emery whistled.

Her horse kicked up her back feet again in a halfhearted leap and then trotted back over to her.

"Come on, you. What's this all about?" She held out her hands. "Back to the stables."

Stargazer nudged her and she laughed again. "I don't even know if you deserve those treats I promised. What's this all about, huh?"

Nash smiled down at her. "You were worried I'd fall off a horse?"

"Well, yeah." She grinned, and then lifted her hurt arm to brush hair out of her face. "Oh ow!" She winced and then cradled it against her.

"That isn't a good sign. Come on now. Let's get you to the doctor."

CHAPTER 15

*M*ama Dawson dug around in her vegetable garden. She had a large one out back, but kept this smaller one with a few of her personal favorites up close to the kitchen. Half the space held herbs—basil, thyme, sage, peppers, onions, garlic. But the other half had a few beet plants for the greens, swiss chard—also for the greens—and two tomato plants. She loved fresh tomatoes.

But no garden survived in Texas without a daily battle against the weeds. And as long as it happened first thing in the morning, Mama was just fine with that. The sun wasn't up. She liked to smell the dirt and the vegetables, and to think.

Billy Thornton had called her again last night. They'd tried the video chat feature and she liked it. He was a good man. Something about his tender insecurity where they were concerned warmed her heart toward him. Tommy had always thought Billy was a good man. He was trusted and liked. And he was highly interested in her.

She'd offered the back bedroom when he came to stay,

and he'd taken her up on it. Something about the whole thing felt fun and new and comforting. But did it feel right?

And that was why she was tugging away at the stubborn weeds with extra gusto this morning. She didn't know if it was right.

Their earlier conversation was replaying through her mind. Billy was a character. And he'd talked to Nash about wanting to court her.

She smiled. It had been a long time since anyone had used the word "courting" around her, and she knew she liked that too. There was lots to like where Billy was concerned.

According to Billy, Nash was all for it, but he warned the poor man about Maverick. She didn't know if it was merited. Would Maverick be unhappy if his mother found another person to share her life with? She didn't really think he would. Sure, it might get complicated. Would they invite Billy in to help run the business? They should. He was smart and he'd been around from the beginning. He knew what Tommy would have wanted, and Billy was adapting to the problems they all faced today.

But did she want to share her life with a new person? A stranger? She tugged at a stubborn root until it ripped out of the earth, flinging a clump of dirt onto her forehead. God had been quiet about Billy. And Mama had to admit she felt selfish. It was so much easier to pray for others, for each of her children, to petition the good Lord to bless them with all they needed. How many hours had she spent praying over their spouses, their future children, their happiness and health? She could do that with full faith the Lord heard her. But now? Was she confused by her own desires? By the way Billy made her feel? She blushed even to herself. She'd dreamt of kissing him last night after their talk.

She jerked some more weeds around, but she was running out of victims to her confusion. The dream was all his fault. He was hinting around about catching her alone in barns and at lookout point and pretending they were college kids again. It had been so funny, she'd cried. But it left her with all sorts of questions and curiosity. What would it be like to kiss another man? Heaven help her.

"I'm sorry, Tommy Dawson. I've been loyal to you my whole life and now here I am, thinking of kissing another man." Mama could hardly say the words out loud. Thank the heavens no one could hear. What would they think of their mother then?

Her heart ached inside for her husband. The pain never left. But somehow, after all these years, she had found room for more. Was it possible to love Tommy still and invite another into her life?

Two years ago—even six months ago—she would have said no, impossible. But now, she was living through the cascading emotions that filled her, and she knew it was most definitely possible.

And what would she do with Billy in her house? Enjoy the man while looking at pictures of her husband, their family pictures over the years? She sat back on her haunches, the entire vegetable garden weed free. After this coming week, she would know one way or the other. It would either be guilt filled and awkward or new and promising. That was all she knew now. If she didn't try, she would never know. And something about Billy Thornton had made her want to try.

Nash had talked to a man who wanted to date his mother, and her son hadn't called her. She wasn't surprised. He called so rarely. But she'd have thought he would have after the talk he apparently had with Billy. But maybe he hoped to keep their business arrangements to themselves. Billy had shared a vague idea of Nash's business plans. Mama approved of his stock management ideas. It was an excellent idea for the Dawson brand to branch out like that. What she hoped for now was a way the younger generations could continue. And Nash was making his way. But this concussion of his. There was no reason for him to have the full investment up front, not if it risked his brain. Mama herself could invest. Mav had offered. The Dawson brand could contribute. They, too, would benefit, and so they should help it get off the ground.

She shook her head, and this time prayed in earnest about Nash. "Please watch over him in his stubbornness. Make a way for him to see clearly and to stop riding. And of course, Thy will be done. Thou sees more than I can."

And now, at the end of the prayer, should she mention her own situation? "About Billy . . ." She waited. She felt normal, so she continued. "He's a good man." Her heart warmed at the thought of him. And she remembered many times they'd interreacted over the years. She thought of his good wife, who had also passed away. She remembered him stepping in so often to help others. And then she thought of his goodness to her, his tender care. "Yes, Billy is a good man. Might I join our lives together? Should I accept his attention and maybe one day marry?" She almost quaked at the thought, but she concentrated on her prayer, and the words felt important and solid. No answers came, but one strong thought did. It wasn't good for her to be alone. It was okay for her to have companionship. For Billy and for her. She sighed. Perhaps God was just letting her know she could decide.

She paused, her heart tightening. She formulated

thoughts for the words she couldn't speak aloud. Her heart clenched and then released, causing an odd heartbeat. *"Will Tommy be sad to see me with another?"* She clutched at her heart, feeling a sense of betrayal. But after a few moments of worry, a great peace filled her. Memories of Tommy also flooded her brain. Their first kiss, the proposal, the birth of Maverick and then each of their children. Their fights and their triumphs. Her life with Tommy rolled over her and peace turned to joy. And love. She felt his love. His hand in hers, his lips on her head, on her neck, on her mouth. His arm around her in bed. The soft scent of his skin. Their moments at work, side by side. And so much more. She wrapped her arms around herself, relishing every second.

His last moments, his kiss on her hand when he was almost too weak to move. "Don't be sad, my Milly. Don't be sad." She'd tried to stop the tears, to smile, but it was too much. "How can I not be sad?"

Even now thinking of it, her tears fell.

"You are my everything," she'd told him.

"I don't want you to be alone." His large palm held the side of her face. She turned into his palm, kissing his hand, then holding it to her chest. And then he was gone.

Remembering those moments, Milly mourned him all over again. "Oh, I miss you. I miss you every moment of every day."

But she stood alone. No one seemed to hear. She'd felt so near him moments ago, and now it was all gone again.

Stunned from her experience, she now felt oddly empty. She stood from her crouched position, her body creaking in all kinds of places. Then she hefted the bucket with all the weeds she'd pulled and made her way to the back garage. She dumped her gloves in the glove drawer, took off her outdoor apron, and then washed her hands in the garage sink. Tommy didn't want her to be alone. She hadn't thought of those words in a long time, had more or less forgotten he'd said them. At the time, she'd assumed that Tommy had been talking about her children. He didn't want her to be alone. Keep the children close. She could keep the family together, have dinners, work to be a unit still. But now she wondered, had he been talking about marrying another?

Her sigh was heavy and long. Time to wash up. No need for anyone to see the signs of her tears.

But as she opened the door, Grace stood in the kitchen as if she was waiting for her. "Oh, Grandma!" She ran and threw her arounds around Mama. "You're sad."

Mama hugged her back. A few more tears resurfaced, but it was more a happy hug. "How grateful I am for your bright light in my life." She patted her sweet, teenaged granddaughter. "How have I been so blessed?"

"I think I'm the blessed one. You were out there weeding? Is that why you were crying?" Grace laughed. "I can weed."

"Oh, there's plenty of weeding. Don't let me stop you if you ever have a hankering. But it wasn't the weeds that brought these tears." She patted her granddaughter's hand. "Come. I think we need to make some sweet lemonade."

"I beat you to it!" Grace laughed again. "Let's have a seat. It must have been hot outside with all that weeding."

Mama followed after her darling granddaughter. "Thank you, my lamb." They sat together on the swing on the back porch. "This is the place I think your parents fell in love." Mama laughed.

"Should we go sit somewhere else?" Grace wrinkled her nose.

But Mama just laughed again. "Your grandpa and I also

144

spent many mornings and evenings sitting right here, and often with a lemonade in our hands." She kicked from the ground, and the swing rocked gently.

"Why are you sad? Do you miss Grandpa?"

She wondered just how much to tell her teenage sidekick. "I've loved you from the moment I saw you." She ran her fingers down Grace's shimmery blond hair. "You've made such a difference in our family. And now we've become partners in a way, haven't we?"

Grace nodded and waited. Mama knew she would have to tell her something. Why not tell her all? This could be a teaching moment.

Mama prided herself in finding teaching moments.

"We have much to discuss. But first I'll talk to you about these tears." She smiled. Grace shifted so she leaned in close, and Mama put an arm round her shoulders. "I'm not sad, exactly, though I did spend some time in the gardens thinking of your grandpa. Did you know that today is the anniversary of his death? He would have loved you. You would have loved him. The two of you would have been peas in a pod, the way you work and your love for animals." She patted Grace on the arm. "But I was also very happy in the gardens. Some of these tears were the happy kind. Sometimes a thing that brings sorrow can also bring joy." She looked out over their backyard, which led to the acreage behind their home. "I'm trying to figure out what God wants me to do."

Grace lifted her head to take a peek into her grandmother's face, but then just sat still, and Mama appreciated that she let her be.

"There's a man . . ."

Grace whipped around, her eyes dancing with delight. "Oh?"

Mama couldn't even stop the blush that filled her face. "Yes. Now, if you're going to get all dramatic about it, I might have to stop."

Grace held up her hands. "Oh, no drama here, Grandma. I'm so here for this news, though." She sat back again, giving Mama such a side-eye that she couldn't help but laugh.

"He's an old family friend, but lately, we talk, and it's nice."

Grace nodded. Mama could tell she was holding back any other comments, but it was taking some difficulty.

"And I think I like him." Mama smiled, eyes brimming again. "He's really wonderful."

Grace sat forward again. "Oh, I'm so happy for you!" She flung her arms around Mama's shoulders and squeezed her tight. "Now, when do I get to meet this man?"

"He's coming to stay with us next week." She held her breath. "Along with Nash and his friend Emery and her sister Lacey." Mama laughed. "It's going to be quite a week."

Grace waved her hands in front of her. "Hold on. Nash has a friend? What kind of friend?" Her mouth twitched like she might not be overly thrilled with the idea.

"Oh, come now. We aren't going to begrudge Nash a little happiness, are we?"

Grace shrugged.

"They aren't really anything yet. But I think they're headed down that path, and she's a wonderful woman and could use a good man like Nash. And I like her. She doesn't let him get away with anything." Mama clasped her hands in her lap. "And Billy will be here with the lot of them." She sighed. "I'd really like things to work out with him."

146

"So what's the dilemma?"

"How can I do something like that to your grandfather? How could I do that to my Tommy? Only, for a moment outside, I think I got my answer. I think he would want me to have somebody."

"You have so many somebodies, Grandma. You have me!" Grace grinned and kissed Mama on the cheek. "But I know what you mean. I'd like to have somebody too."

"Oh, you will. Don't be rushing into that too quickly." Mama squeezed her tight. "So that's all. When I asked God what to do, I just had a flood of memories." She considered her thoughts. "But one very important one." She sighed. "It still doesn't calm the sorrow that comes from moving on. Isn't that something? I have hope and sorrow at the same time. Joy and mourning. Whoever thought a person could have all that emotion swirling about at once?"

"Oh, believe me, I know what you mean there."

Mama laughed. "Let's finish these lemonades. I think we have a bit of work to do for your and Nash's project, don't we?"

"Yes! And I have news. We have another sponsor."

They began to talk about Willow Creek Days and all the many details that still needed ironing out. It was an excellent conversation, during which they went inside and unloaded the dishwasher and cut up the vegetables for that evening's soup. Somewhere in the middle, Grace suddenly reached out her arm to hug Mama again. "I think you deserve every happiness. If you want to have someone, you should have them."

And with those words and the huge influx of peace in Mama's heart, she knew her granddaughter was right.

CHAPTER 16

The doctor did not bring good news for Emery. After the initial diagnosis of a fracture, a couple weeks later, and she was still talking about possible surgery. Minimally, she had a fracture in the bone right below her shoulder, and was not supposed to ride for at least six weeks. Worst case scenario? Surgery with eight-to-ten-week recovery times.

Nash drove her back to their trailers. She was quiet. Too quiet. And he wasn't sure how to help her. He opened his mouth to say something, anything, multiple times but ended up closing it again and sat in further silence.

"Stop, please." She looked out the window.

"I'm literally doing nothing."

"You're over there feeling sorry for me. Just say what you want to say." She glanced at him, her frown growing.

"I don't want to say anything, otherwise I would. You're a little scary right now."

She looked away. "I don't expect you to understand."

He snorted.

"What's that snort supposed to mean?"

"Why wouldn't I understand? I'm in literally the same situation you are."

She crossed her arms. "Are you? Because last I checked, if you don't make any money at all in rodeo, you still have a place to live and a family." Her mouth turned down, but she was not finished. "If I can't ride, I can't eat. And if I lose that sponsorship before I even get it . . . again, I won't have anything else to fall back on. This is it for me."

Nash felt many things at once, one he wasn't particularly proud of. He'd done everything he could to stand on his own two feet, and he didn't need Emery throwing back the Dawson family in his face. He didn't take money from them. He didn't want them involved. He was a contributor. And he was tired of everyone thinking otherwise. All the pent-up years of frustration were bubbling to the surface, and he worked hard to tamp them down. She was in a tough situation. And he had never ever worried about his next meal, not really. It was different, knowing Mama had food in her kitchen. "I know. You're right. But just because I have a fall-back doesn't mean I ever plan to use it. I plan to make my own way and contribute to the Dawson brand or not be a part of it." He stopped at the stop sign and then moved forward through town.

"I get that. But trust me, you don't understand. And you can't really. You've never been in my situation."

He would never understand with complete empathy what Emery was going through. But he could sure as heck try, and he knew what it felt like to be disappointed. And if she thought that his head wasn't aching half the time and he wasn't trying to pretend like everything was great when it wasn't and that his career wasn't also probably over when he needed just a few more bucks for his whole life plan to work . . . well, if she thought he didn't have anything to complain about, she had another thing coming.

But he kept these thoughts to himself, except to say, "I'm sorry. What are you going to do?"

"I'm riding." She shrugged. "I'll take some pain relievers and ride. And we're going to Willow Creek this next week, and I'll ride there too."

"I'll be back up on a bull at home." He shrugged too. "Sounds like we're both as stubborn as the other."

"Fine. But I can't afford not to. And you can. So we can both be stubborn, but our situations are not the same."

Nash could not understand why she was so adamantly repeating how her situation was unique, but there was something in her eyes, a desperation and a fear that he knew he'd never felt. And so he reached for her hand. "I'm really sorry." This time he meant the words more. "I'm a stranger to that fear you have. I would like to try and ease it. You have friends. You have opportunities." *You have me!* He wanted to emphasize that he was in her life, in a new yet devoted way. "I'll be there for you. And let's talk about it at the Dawson dinner table." He winked. "A lot of problems get solved at that table."

Emery nodded, her eyes lighting back up again. A darker cloud still marred some of their brilliance, but at least the hope returned.

"And hey, as long as you don't fall off Stargazer, you should be fine."

"I could say the same for you . . . oh wait. You fall off a bull every single time." She mock-scowled at him. "Does your mama know your situation?"

"Yes, of course she knows. That woman always knows."

"And she's okay with you riding?"

"Probably not, but she's also okay with letting me navigate my own mistakes."

Emery laughed. "I like this woman."

"She's really special." He turned into the rodeo grounds. "So, your medical history is private. Billy is not entitled to know and neither is Isaiah. What would you like me to say about it?"

"That you don't know the specifics. I'll handle the rest."

"Very good." Nash still had hold of her hand, so he laced their fingers. "Want to come to my place tonight? Watch a movie?" He kissed the back of her hand.

She swallowed very obviously and then nodded, her gaze glued to his mouth on her knuckle.

So he smiled and kissed another one. "I could kiss you all day, you know. We could go find someplace quiet . . ." He nipped the next knuckle with his teeth. But then he released her. "Except that I agreed to help with more chores. And Lacey said she'd be my partner."

"What are you doing?"

"Mucking out the stables."

Emery's grin started small, but then she let it fill her face, her laugh following. "This I gotta see."

"I'll snag a few pics."

"Excellent. I'll stop by if I can. I've got to make some phone calls first."

He wanted to know what those phone calls were about but he let her be. She hopped out of the truck, wincing as her arm brushed the door.

But he didn't mention it. She was tough. And she didn't

want attention brought to her arm. Hopefully she had some solid pain medications.

In the meantime, working on the last week of his mandatory four-week break was near gonna kill him. But at least they had Willow Creek to look forward to, and Emery at his house. He grinned, watching her step up inside her trailer. He wasn't sure how it happened, but at least they'd gone from being an itch to an embrace. He'd take that even over a healed head, and that was saying something.

The week passed slower than a big mama sow getting up from her morning nap. Nash was about ready to kick the whole thing to the curb by the time he closed up his trailer for the week. But Lacey and Emery exiting at the same time helped him put the whole thing behind him.

"You pretty ladies ready for some of God's finest country?"

"You bet we are!" Lacey held up her arms and danced.

He tossed their bags into the back of his truck and held the door open for them to climb on in. "I hope you like Bob Dylan . . ."

"What? No way." Lacey shook her head and leaned across Emery to reach the radio. "I'll be taking care of music." With her phone already plugged into the system, she began scrolling through tunes.

Emery sat at his side. With one arm around her and another on the wheel, he glanced behind them to back up. "I think I'm gonna like this week."

Emery leaned her head against his shoulder and nodded. She was quiet, but Nash knew she had a lot on her mind.

As the Texas countryside flew by them, Nash knew he could spend many hours just like they were and be one happy man.

But could they do so? A week in Willow Creek was going to tell him all he needed to know about his future in every way possible. His career. Joining forces with Billy, his mother's relationship with the man, Mav's opinions about it all, and his future with Emery all sort of hung in the balance of the results from this one week.

CHAPTER 17

*F*or the next few weeks, Emery was as happy as it was possible to be while still knowing that she risked her arm and livelihood every time she rode. But even so, happiness was possible and she felt it deeply, especially riding in the truck next to Nash. They were heading to his home, but now hers too. She'd made the leap and told the Realtor to begin the process of purchasing the land. During the conversation, she'd asked where it sat compared to the Dawson land and had to laugh out loud when she heard it was down the street.

"You'll sit in the opposite valley. A ridge separates the two properties, but the road cuts through that geography, and you're three mailboxes away."

Emery smiled thinking about it. She hadn't told Nash yet. They were so new. And he'd obviously felt constricted by the news the first time she mentioned it. But she could live wherever she wanted to, and she'd taken the steps to do so. She had a down payment, but not enough to invest in the startup of livestock or any of the things that would earn her the money to keep the house. That would come. She'd taken the leap. And she knew it would come. If not, property was as easy to sell as it was to buy apparently, at least in Willow Creek. Her heart ached to keep it, though. It was her very dream.

And then when she at last settled down with a family, she would have something to give them: a lovely place to grow up.

Nash lifted his hand from around her back and then turned down the long drive to the Dawson house. "Home sweet home." He leaned his head down on top of hers for the briefest second, and that felt so nice. So warm. Was she coming home?

They pulled into view of the farmhouse, and her heart melted and then soared. "It's the most beautiful thing I've ever seen." Tears immediately came to her eyes.

Lacey patted her arm. "Are you crying?"

Nash looked down. "You are?" He stopped the car partway down the drive. "Are you okay?"

"Oh, she's fine. She's just looking at her dream." Lacey waved her fingers, as if it weren't one of the most significant moments in Emery's life.

She swallowed, forcing down a sharp lump that crowded her throat. "I love it." She nodded. "It's perfect."

Nash kissed the top of her head. "You make a man real glad for his upbringing. No wonder my mama loves you."

She gasped. "She is too good. Oh, I hope I'm not an imposition. Are you sure you have room?"

"Oh, we have room." He pointed to the upstairs. "Mama's only happy when each of those rooms has someone sleeping in it."

Emery hoped that was true. She'd met Mama before and

had talked to her a bit regarding the Willow Creek Days rodeo, but she wouldn't say she knew the woman, and she'd felt almost guilty accepting her offer to stay at the house, but she could not resist.

"I think I might have a difficult time leaving this place." She sighed, then side-eyed Nash, who hadn't stiffened up or panicked or anything.

"I like the sound of that."

"Do you?" She looked deep into his eyes and could see no sign of insincerity.

"Yep, now come on. Let's get you inside your dream."

She laughed. "You joke, but this is real."

"I'm not making light of your dream. Go on in. I'll grab the bags." He'd pulled up to the very front by then.

Lacey hopped out and Emery followed. The side yard led to a white picket fence running from the front of the property to the back. A few horses munched on grass toward the other side of the fence. A couple dogs came running around the side of the house, but they ignored Emery and Lacey and dove at Nash.

He laughed, holding all their bags. "Princess! Hello! Who's my cute puppy? Who's my cute dog?" He kept walking, and the dogs bounded around him like they couldn't get enough.

Emery smiled. They stepped up onto the front porch. It was wide and long and looked like it wrapped around the whole house. The front door had beautiful etched glass. Above it hung a sign. "Welcome in Christ."

"I've never seen that before." Emery pointed.

Lacey nodded, and lifted her hand as if to knock.

"Oh, just go on in," Nash called from behind them.

But the door opened and Mrs. Dawson smiled at them. "Well hello! This must be Lacey, Emery's sister. And Emery herself. And there's my Nash." She glowed with all the smiles and glee you would expect from a woman who had been awaiting their arrival for weeks on end.

The love washed over Emery like a rainfall in the desert. She couldn't get enough. But it didn't feel fleeting. It settled itself deep inside. Emery was pulled into a warm, soft hug, the kind that left a mark. "I'm so happy you're here, my dear," Mrs. Dawson said. "Welcome."

She did the same to Lacey, and Emery's heart melted again, watching her sister feel love from a motherly figure besides herself. She'd never been able to be a Mama Dawson to Lacey, but she'd done her best. It wasn't too late. They were moving to this town. Lacey could see what a real family looked like. Something didn't sit right with that thought. She and Lacey were family, no matter what. But Emery wanted her to have more.

Mrs. Dawson stepped back so they could come in. She kissed Nash's cheek. "Put those bags in the yellow room and then come right back. I've got to hug you properly." She patted his arm.

"Yes, ma'am." He stepped past and headed toward the stairs. The dogs had stayed outside, but they both sat, watching the front door like Nash might emerge any minute.

Mrs. Dawson just laughed. "Oh, those two. Nash will go out and play fetch and they'll be as happy as can be. They're supposed to be working."

"Your dogs work?" Lacey had a look of wonder about her that Emery hoped stuck around.

"You bet. They keep predators off the property and keep the herds gathered. Plus they give all the visitors the welcome they deserve." She smiled. "Come into the kitchen. I have some lemonade and so much to talk about." Her smile grew wider as she leaned closer. "Especially before Nash gets back down those stairs."

"I can hear you, Mama, and I'm back. And I'd love some of that lemonade." He draped an arm over Emery's shoulders. "You're not the only one who appreciates this woman right here."

Mama's eyes warmed and she nodded. "I'm pleased to see you've got some good sense in there with all those good looks."

Emery laughed. "Maybe it was the concussion."

Mama burst out laughing, and Nash shook his head, turning to her. "You saying I got sense knocked into me? Is that what you're saying?"

She shrugged. "I'm not saying anything."

Mama waved them in. "Come. Grace and I made extra lemonade the other day and then some more fresh last night. It's especially sweet."

Nash opened the fridge and pulled out a huge pitcher. "Mama makes the best."

"And Grace too."

"Where is my little scallywag?"

"Oh, she's off at school. Or at the barn. I never can keep track of her schedule. But as soon as she can, she'll be barreling you over, don't worry about that. That girl can't wait to see you."

"You trying to tell me her pig isn't company enough?" Nash laughed.

"Nope, nor any of her many beaus."

Nash stopped. "Her beaus?" He didn't smile. His eyes had gone steely. And Emery decided she liked the protective side of him, liked it a whole lot.

"Oh, don't you worry about her. She has a great head on

her shoulders. And a dad who is already protective enough for a whole choir of women." Mama waved her hand. "Now stop with that and be happy for the girl."

"I am, believe me." Nash rotated his shoulders. "I want to show Em around. Anything happening for the next couple hours?"

"Not a thing. You two go have fun. You might want to check out the other side of the ridge too." She winked at Emery, who widened her eyes. Did Mama know everything?

"I'd like that," Emery chimed in.

Nash shrugged. "Both sides of the ridge, it is."

As they were walking out, Mama laughed to herself a minute before pulling Lacey aside. "Have you ever made bread?"

Emery was loving every minute. As soon as the door shut behind them, she sighed. "I'm so happy for Lacey. This is incredible for her."

Nash took her hand. "I'm just happy for me." He swung their hands together. "Is that selfish?"

"In this case, not at all." She grinned. "But I'm completely biased." They stepped along the back porch, past a large swing. "Oh, we need to put in some time on this swing."

"Done. And you have to see the barn loft." He wiggled his eyebrows.

But she stopped, tugging him. "We are not visiting all your old make-out locations." She shook her head.

"Fine, loft is out. But can we make some new ones?" His eyes widened in mock innocence.

"Of course." She skipped, and then winced. "Dang. I forget I have a broken arm."

"You could put it in a sling." Nash seemed to brace himself for her reaction.

"Nah. I don't want everyone knowing. They'll be loving and good and try to talk me out of riding. But this week is important for the sponsors and for me. We're the king and queen, right?" She laughed. "What is that going to do to your reputation around here?"

"Hopefully, it will completely elevate things. I'm in need of a reputation overhaul."

She laughed. "Should we ride our horses?"

"They won't arrive until later this afternoon, I don't think, but we have a barn full of them. Let's get ourselves all saddled up."

Emery squeezed his hand as they walked along. "I just keep thinking it's all going to disappear. That if I let go, you'll be gone, and all of this will fade away." She shivered. "Tell me it's real."

Nash stopped in the middle of the back gardens and pulled her into his arms. "I don't know much about too many things. I mess up trying to talk to you all the time. I really am just making things up as I go along. But this right here, me and you, is real for me. It's the realest thing I've ever had, and I'm not letting go." He raised his chin. "Stubborn, remember?"

Her hands ran up his chest to his shoulders, searching, always looking to see if he meant what he said. She should just believe the man. Maybe she could. His eyes stared down at her, their deep blue going on forever deeper and more brilliantly into his soul. She nodded. "This is real for me too."

His arms circled around her tighter, bringing her closer. "I've never made out with anyone in the middle of my mom's gardens before."

She laughed, and then shook her head. "Maybe we'll find a different spot."

"Maybe just a quick one?" His eyebrow rose, and then he closed the distance and placed a soft, intense, inviting kiss on her mouth, so delicious, she leaned into him.

"More? Later?" Nash winked.

She could only nod again.

They swung hands, forward and back, linked together, down to the barn.

The horses were glorious. Well taken care of, shiny coats, pleased to be out riding. Emery found herself more and more in love with everything around them. One of the first places he took them was the highest point on the property, the southern ridge. Their horses climbed it easily. The cedar trees and the pines dotted the forest around them. The brush was full and the path well used. After a gentle ride up to the ridge, the wind picked up and they walked to the edge.

Rolling hills, rocky ridges, and green stretched out in every direction. It was divided by white fences, and houses dotted the hills. The sky was blue and stretched in all directions to the very horizon. The air smelled of earth and sage and cedar. Emery held her arms out to her sides and closed her eyes. "Can we fly? Tell me we can fly!" She laughed.

"We can!" Nash's eyes were on her. She could feel them. Her skin tingled as though brushed by his gaze. She let his attention, his assurance, his interest fill her, and then she opened her eyes.

"So tell me about those properties down on this side of the ridge. Your mama was talking about us riding over there too, right?"

"Yep, she was." Nash pursed his lips. "We don't own any of that land, but it gets some really great irrigation. The stock does well down there, plenty to eat."

"Oh?" She couldn't keep the excitement out of her face.

"Do you have a particular interest?" He watched her. "You do. And Mama knows." He shook his head. "Why am I the last to know in our threesome?"

"Well, you knew I was interested in land here."

"True, but specific land? Land right there across this ridge?"

Emery laughed. "Last time I told you about any of this, you freaked out."

"I did not freak out." He ran a hand through his hair. "I think this is great. Tell me."

"Well, I need you to help me figure out which one from here, but I put an offer on a house down the street from you." She held her breath and then turned to him.

But this time, his face filled with wonder. "Did you now?"

"Yes I did."

"Now, that might be the best news I've heard in a long time."

Some relief in his reaction added to her hope. "I'm pretty excited about it. I can't afford any of the things I need to start the business yet, but it does have a hay crop, and that might help me get started." She shrugged. "Now, tell me which one."

He laughed. "Well, I can't be sure. How many mailboxes down?"

"Mama said three."

"That woman has her ways."

"So where is it?" She leaned forward, as if getting a few inches closer was going to help her solve the mystery of which property was hers.

"Three houses down. That's the Goldsteins' property!" Nash nodded. "That's prime real estate. It has the largest section of the river that runs down these hills through the properties. And the widest expanse for pasture land." He

163

eyed her appraisingly. "An out of towner with that good of an eye is an impressive thing indeed." He pointed toward the road. "Many might be confused by the narrow piece along the road. And the house is smaller. But this is one of the best properties around, especially if you want to raise stock, or even the hay crops too." He tipped his imaginary hat. "Nice work, Em."

"We'll see what happens. I'll hear back from the bank and our Realtor this week."

He shifted. "Let's get going on this tour. I want to see the property." His eagerness made her smile.

"Me too." She laughed.

Nash gave her a galloping, wild tour of the Dawson property, and then they headed down the street to cross the ridge. He sat so easy in the saddle, he looked born to ride. Emery loved that look most about him. They couldn't run the horses on the dirt road, so they just eased up, but it wouldn't be far. And she wanted to see everything about the road between her house and the Dawsons'.

They street was lined with trees, and grass along the road. They approached the first mailbox. A burst of bluebonnets filled the grassy area in front. "Oh lovely!"

Nash nodded. "Mama started a neighborhood effort to plant more bluebonnets. She'll be happy to hear about this." He whipped out his phone and snatched a picture. Then he pointed in her direction and snapped one super-fast.

"Wait, I wasn't even smiling. What if I look terrible?"

"You don't."

"You didn't even look at it."

"I don't need to." He smiled. "I just want to remember you up there on that horse, walking along my street. It's doing things to me." He laughed. "Good things."

Emery couldn't prevent the smile and then the laugh. "Well, all right, then." She snapped a picture of him. "Seeing you up on a horse is doing things to me too."

"Fair."

They came up on the next mailbox, and more bluebonnets. "I'm so excited about all of this. I don't even know what to do with myself."

Her horse danced underneath her.

"Well, Powder there wants to ride."

"I know. Do you think we can ride out on the property?"

"Of course. If the Goldsteins are home, we'll just ask; if they aren't, they won't mind. And we can send over one of Mama's pies. That appeases all unhappy neighbors."

She nodded. "I'll have to remember that."

"Oh? Do you make pie?"

Nash's overly hopeful grin sent another wave of pleased tickles through her center. "I do." But she clamped her lips, and then her full attention was devoted to the next bit of property. The trees lightened and the land opened up as an expanse of grass filed her view. The fence along the front was well taken care of. And the bluebonnets were more sparse over here, but they would spread. They rode along in silence as she took in every detail. "It's beautiful." She choked. "I can hardly speak."

"You don't need to." He nodded.

They entered through the main gate and walked down the front lane. It was narrower in front, and the home was not visible yet. But as they turned a corner through trees, it opened up again to a little cottage-type home in the center of more trees. If she were to describe it, she might have used the word magical. For it looked to be right out of a storybook.

"They aren't here. At least their trucks aren't."

They hopped off the horses and left the reins resting on the porch railing. Nash took the porch steps in one bound and rapped on the door quickly.

After a few minutes, and no one coming to the door, they grabbed their horses and walked around the house toward the back. "They have a barn back here. And their fields go out behind the house and off to the left for many miles. Really, it's beautiful." Nash's voice had a hint of longing, which surprised Emery. Didn't he already have property? He'd been raised on land just like this. But the more she thought about Nash and his situation and what he'd said earlier about making his own way, she could tell that he, too, wanted land. He wanted what Emery was buying. And that made her yearn to share it with him.

But she didn't say anything about it. That was silly. And if he wanted to be in her life to that degree, much more would need to happen. She would have to be in love, for one, and he would need to propose and so many other things. She tried to calm the heat she felt in her face, but knew it was impossible. The thought of pursuing something more serious with Nash was simply such a profound thought, she couldn't dismiss it. But she couldn't speak it either.

So she focused all her new emotion toward the land, though now it was linked forever in her mind with Nash.

They exited through the yards closer to the house. They held a chicken coop complete with chickens, free-range wandering in a covered, fenced structure. And a pond. And many gardens, overflowing with vegetables. And down around the next corner, a greenhouse. Very small, but full of green, and flowers as well.

Emery held a hand at her neck.

The outbuildings were neat but a bit rundown. Nothing a little mending couldn't take care of. And she wanted to squeal. She would have actual outbuildings. Then they moved toward the back gate.

"Out there is the larger pasture lands and the grazing lands, and some of their hay crops." Nash nodded in that direction. "Would you like to ride out across them all?"

"Yes!" She laughed. "Unless you're ready to get back."

"Not at all." He hopped down and handed her the reins to his horse. Then he opened the gate and bowed to her. "My lady."

She dipped her head. "Thank you, good sir." Then she laughed.

He swung back on the gate to send it closed and clipped it shut. Then leapt up on his horse. She tossed him the reins and knew he was about to take off like a madman.

So she joined him.

The first pasture blurred by in shadows of yellow, green, and soft earth. Nash took the lead, pointing down toward a green, tree-filled gulley.

Emery followed, and when he slowed down, she did too.

"Those are pecans right there, just growing wildly by the water source." A lovely river rushed by. "It's much higher now from recent rains. You'll always have water in this thing, but not this much."

She nodded, and then let her horse go to the water for a drink.

They both hopped down, and Nash immediately took her hand. "This is amazing. Everything about this." They stood in the shade. Filtered sunlight touched their skin and a soft breeze off the water cooled them a bit. He pulled her closer.

"So you don't mind if I'm your neighbor?"

He shook his head. "I'm thinking about moving in." Her eyes widened, but he didn't seem to notice. "This right here looks like the perfect place to park my trailer."

She laughed overly loud to cover her misunderstanding. "Oh right. Yeah. Well, you're welcome anytime."

"I'm really happy for you." He tucked her hair behind her left ear and then ran his hands down her arms. "You and Lacey deserve this. It's gonna work out. And we will help."

She nodded. "I hope it will. It's just so wonderful, I'm still fearing it won't last. That something is gonna happen to take it away. Is that so negative of me?"

"Not at all. But it will work. When will you hear back?"

"Tomorrow, I think."

"We'll have a celebration when you do."

She smiled. "Thank you. For all of this, for not freaking out about me moving into your hometown. Well, I guess, only freaking out a little bit."

"I'm telling you, that was not a freak out. At all. I didn't even say anything."

Emery laughed and then dipped her fingers into the water. "It's so nice."

"There's a swimming hole up on our property."

"And I hear there's one up a different ridge too." She wiggled her eyebrows.

"True! It's pretty populated with all my old high school flings."

She wrinkled her nose. "Maybe we'll just stick around here."

"Good call. Though I wouldn't mind showing you off a little bit."

"I think we'll get plenty of press when we ride in together on horses." She made a little face.

"You embarrassed to be seen with me?" Nash held a hand to his chest.

"No. Not at all, just thinking you might be feeling some of that." She threw some water in his direction, adding a mist of droplets to his arms. "Not that I won't be an asset to your brand or anything. Can you imagine all my riders drooling over you?" She tossed some more water, this time getting the front of his shirt.

"Hey now. Like my bull-riding fanatics aren't gonna be eyeing you standing next to me." He lowered his hand in the water. "You sure you want to start something right now?"

She scooted away. "Of course not." But then she really dug in and doused him with a huge splash of water.

"What, you did not!" He cupped large amounts of water, sending it all over her. She was drenched before she could escape out into the sun. She kept running, the feel of its warmth on her wet skin nice, until she was in the center of a hayfield and golden fronds stretched in every direction for thirty feet or more.

Nash joined her.

"You gotta admit, this is pretty cool," Emery said.

"Want to know what's even cooler?"

She nodded.

He stomped on some hay, flattening a space for them, and lay down, his hands behind his head. "This."

She joined him.

The sky was a vivid blue, the brightness of the sun blocked by the hay around them—everything blocked by that hay. The sweet smell filled her senses, and the softness beneath her was welcoming and comfortable.

"It's so quiet," she whispered.

Nash seemed to listen. "That's what I love most about a good hayfield."

They lay side by side, her head on his shoulder, and Emery listened to the silence. And somewhere deep inside, things started to go quiet even in her mind, until her breaths and Nash's heartbeat were all that she heard.

And it was getting louder and more rapid.

He shifted, and suddenly, she was much more aware of Nash than anything else around her. His strong thigh was pressed up against hers. His arm cradled her. His chin moved so that it rested on the top of her head.

So she turned toward him and placed her hand on his chest. His heart hammered beneath her fingertips. She lifted her head, asking to ease her suspicions, "What's the other thing you like to do in hayfields?"

"The only thing I've ever done in a hayfield is hide and listen to the silence, but . . ."

She smiled. "But?"

"But I could think of a few other things I might like to do here."

"So this would be a new memory?" She sat up on her elbows, looking almost down into his face.

"Everything with you is a new memory, Em. You wipe out all the other parts of my life as if they never happened. But yes. This is the first time I've ever been in a hayfield horizontal, with a woman."

She laughed. "Do I take all the romance out of everything?"

"No way." He reached over and tugged at her ponytail holder. It fell out easily, slipping off her straight hair. "This is glorious." He ran his fingers through the strands, gently avoiding every knot.

A shower of tingles raced over her head and she moaned. "Oh, that's the best. Don't stop, ever."

His laugh was low and soft. "You sure about that?" He moved from her hair to her scalp, running his fingers along her skin underneath the hair, sending trails of happiness all along her head. "Okay, now don't stop doing that." She laughed.

But after a moment, his glorious scalp massage wasn't nearly enough. She lifted her chin up to see him. His eyes were brilliant, reflecting the glow in the sky, smiling at her.

He inched forward, sitting up on his elbow so that he faced her, and then dipped his mouth closer to hers. "How about this?"

She rose up to meet his lips, capturing them immediately, completely, with her own. Her hand went to his hair, pulling him closer as she scooched nearer. But he cradled her with his arms and then held her close. He kissed her again and again, his teeth taking a turn to nibble her lower lip, his mouth pulling at her upper lip until she was gloriously and furiously craving his every touch.

But he paused, kissed her softly once more, and then raised himself back to his elbow. "I think haystacks are now my new favorite place to kiss you."

She noticed he didn't say "kiss a woman," and that made her smile. A glorious sort of satisfaction that Nash might not be wishing to kiss anyone else filled her with confidence. She tipped toward him. "I found a new thing you should definitely not stop."

His smile grew, and she closed the distance between them again, pressing her lips against his, taking the lead. She leaned into him, lifted a hand behind his neck, and kissed him like she had something to say.

And she did. She kissed all her appreciation into him, her gratitude, her happiness, and her desire. It burned within her. He was all man, a cowboy in the purest sense, and everything she'd ever wanted. Even when he chapped her hide like no one else, he was a man to be reckoned with, and she wanted to reckon. She knew with Nash, she was safe. A great feeling of closeness and peace filled her. She slowed her kisses and savored his taste, his soft mouth and the firmness with which he matched each new pressure. He ran his hand down her back and then back up, his fingers toying with the softness of the skin at her neck. But like every good kiss, she knew when it was time to pause. They both did. She rested against him. One last kiss, tugging on his lip, and then she pressed her forehead into his.

"You, woman." He closed his eyes.

"Hmm." She sat back and tucked her knees to her chest.

He lay back beside her, his glorious body stretched out next to her in the hay. "Why haven't we been doing this for the last two years?"

Emery laughed at his question. What a perfect thing to say. "Because I was too dang stubborn to just admit I liked you?"

"Or I was too dang afraid to try anything?"

She peered over at him. "Or it was just not the right time. Everything happens when it does for a reason. And this is going to sound strange, but knowing you all these years, all our silly fights, makes me trust you more than I would if we'd just started talking."

"I definitely know what pushes your buttons." He smirked.

"In more ways that one." She rocked so that she bumped into him.

His laugh filled the air around them. "I love this side of you. You're just so much more than I ever hoped." He laced their fingers again. "And this." He lifted their joined hands. "I have never held a woman's hand so much. It's like I can't be by you without some kind of connection." His face colored just a bit, enough that Emery wanted to kiss him all over again.

"I love it." She ran a thumb along his skin. "And I love hayfields. You know, this will be my field in a few months."

"That's just so incredible. All this will be yours." He sat up. "Have you figured out what kind of stock you're gonna start with?"

They started talking business, and Emery found something she might like just as much as kissing Nash, and that was planning out her business and her life with him.

Hours went by, and the sky was dimming before they stood, stretching out their limbs.

Nash shook his head. "And we aren't nearly finished."

She shrugged. "At least we have lots of time."

A pair of headlights turned on, shining in their faces.

CHAPTER 18

$\mathcal{N}$ash shielded his face. "Hey, turn those off."

They did, and as Nash suspected, he and Emery now faced the other Dawson brothers. "Brace yourself," he murmured.

Mav raised a hand. "Hey. Mama says it's time for dinner."

Nash stood stiffly. "Oh yeah? And did she also tell you where to find us?"

Dylan laughed. "Actually, she did."

"To be clear, she didn't mention the hayfield. We guessed that on our own." Decker's smug smile made Emery laugh.

Well, at least she thought they were funny.

That made one of them. Nash sighed. "Emery Banks, these are my brothers. Maverick, Dylan, and Decker." He pointed to the lineup and indicated they should start walking out of the hay using the small path they had created going in.

Deck snorted. "You've got a bit of hay . . ." He indicated his hair.

Emery ran fingers through hers. "I imagine I have hay everywhere."

Nash just shook his head while all his brothers acted like twelve-year-olds. "I promise they're decent guys. They just sort of forgot how at the moment."

As soon as they were standing closer, Nash whistled for the horses.

"Oh, they came home hours ago." Mav smiled. And then he held out his hand to Emery. "I'm happy to meet you. Mama says you're one in a million and we should count our lucky stars you decided to come be with us despite knowing Nash."

"Did she say all that?" Emery laughed.

"Well, most of it. I threw in the Nash part." He winked.

She shook his hand and the twins' as well. "I'm so happy to meet you all. There's not a rodeo I ever go to where people don't know the Dawson brothers."

Mav clapped Decker on the back. "Then we're doing our job in advertising. The brand is growing."

Nash and Emery shared a look. They'd talked a bit about just that. "Emery put an offer down on this property. We're just about to be neighbors."

Maverick's eyebrows rose. "Well, that's excellent news. Welcome to Willow Creek."

"Thank you."

They climbed into the back of the truck, sitting shoulder to shoulder with Dylan and Decker. Mav drove in the cab alone.

Nash's brothers soon had Emery laughing, and he relaxed a bit more. This visit home would be easier than he thought, maybe, even though he cared more than most visits. After that kiss in the hay, he didn't think he could let go of Emery anytime soon. But who knew what she would think after a whole week with his family. Mav could charm anyone, but he kept his charm at bay when talking to Nash. He shifted in the truck bed.

Emery bumped his shoulder. "You all right?"

Their eyes met, and in hers, he felt like he belonged. He grinned. "Oh yeah, now I am." He laced their fingers together and ignored the pointed looks from his brothers.

They would give it up in a minute. And everyone could just ease into Emery being a normal part of their household this week. And for much longer, he hoped.

Dylan's boots almost touched Emery's thigh. They were stretched out all along the bed. The truck went down in a pothole and everyone rolled into each other, first in one direction and then the other.

"Hey, you dolt. You just wiped your boot on Emery's shirt." Decker whacked his brother with his hat.

She held up her hands. "It's all right. I'm not afraid of a little dirt."

Deck tipped his hat to her. "No, and while we're on the subject, you're also the world-record holder in barrel racing."

"I am. Though I have no idea what that has to do with getting my shirt dirty."

"Oh, everything. It means you aren't afraid of a little work."

Nash nodded approvingly. No, she wasn't. His Emery was not afraid of work. "Don't let her sister fool you. Lacey and I were mucking out stables right before we came. She was raised on the rodeo grounds."

"She and Mama produced some good-looking bread too. Which we can't eat until we bring the two of you back."

"Ah, I see why we got the full brother welcome."

"Yep, we're hungry, and you're the only thing standing between us and a thick, buttered slice of Mama's bread."

Emery stood up. "Then by all means, we have to get this truck moving." She gripped the front of the truck cab and banged on the roof. "Let's go! That bread ain't getting any warmer."

The brothers behind her laughed and then yelped into the air.

They only had another corner to round, but Mav stepped on the gas, a big dust cloud swirling out behind them. Then he slowed when they entered the drive.

Before long, they were all hugging and greeting each other in the front room when a knock sounded at the front door.

"I'll grab that," Grace called.

But Mama shook her head, wiping her hands down the front of her apron. "No, I got it, but could you untie me, dear?"

Something passed between the two of them. And Nash knew it must be Billy. He followed a few steps behind.

Billy's large bulk filled the porch. Nash stepped back to give them a moment. Their soft murmurs together made him smile.

When he rejoined the others, many eyes turned to him, but he just shrugged. And then shortly after, Mama and Billy stepped into the room, and every eye turned there. Nash held out his hand. "Billy! So good to see you. Glad you're here."

The man pulled him into a bear hug like no other, and for a moment, Nash just enjoyed a strong man giving him some love. It had been a long time. And when they separated, his eye might have been a bit misty. "Thank you, man," he said.

"I'm looking forward to more conversations. I've had some ideas since we talked."

"Glad to hear it. I have too." Nash glanced at Emery. Lots of ideas.

The other brothers shook hands. No more hugs went round. And Nash was happy to see that Mav seemed perfectly pleased with the situation.

At last, Mama waved them all toward the dining room. "Let's eat."

Everyone sat in their usual chairs. But another had been added next to Nash. He sat taller, glancing around the table at each of his brothers and their wives, at Billy on the right of Mama. No one had suggested he sit in Dad's chair on the opposite end of the table. Mav sometimes sat there. Especially when they had meetings. But judging by Mama's hand that had not left Billy's, she was perfectly happy to have him at her side.

Nash could appreciate that. A new man in the family—not the head, but a support to Mama, who still functioned as the head of their group.

Mav's eyes went between the two. His wife, Bailey, put a hand on his arm. And Grace nodded at him with a smile. The women in his life were really working on him.

To give him credit, Maverick was an amazing man. He'd loved his wife for years, even after she left him at the altar, even after she disappeared; when she returned, he welcomed her back. He was a good man, and had saved his wife and family because of it.

Dylan and Faith were the sweetest of the group. She was born and raised right here and they were loved by all. Deck and Kate had an interesting beginning, but most of the family considered her to be responsible for saving him from a fate worse than death. A marriage to a woman who did not appreciate him like they hoped one might. He found Kate in

New York, and the two traveled there often, as well as to other locations, for work. He'd created his own consulting firm on top of running much of the business side of the Dawson brand. Nash looked at each person in turn, and his heart did that warming, happy feeling that often happened when he was with family, only this time, it was not accompanied by a ping of loneliness. This time, he had Emery at his side.

She reached for his hand, as if she knew his thoughts were directed at her. "This is the most incredible thing I've ever seen."

Lacey leaned forward next to Emery. "Wow, thanks for having us."

Then Mama sat taller in her seat, and everyone quieted.

"We would like to welcome some new family into our midst."

Emery sucked in a breath.

"Everyone we invite to our table is our family."

"Whether you like it or not." Deck laughed.

"We are pleased to have Emery Banks and her sister Lacey with us. They are here for Willow Creek Days and at my invitation." Her eyes twinkled. "And as our new neighbors. Emery's placed an offer on the Goldstein place."

The women who hadn't heard that particular news erupted in excited chatter. Bailey pointed in the direction of Emery's new home. "I love that place. When do you move in?"

"We're going to have to have a housewarming party for her." Faith grinned. "The ladies in town are going to love you."

Mama continued. "I feel like our Emery and Lacey already belong. And we thank you for being here with us."

Her smiled turned tender. "And this is Billy Thornton. I know you all know him. He was a friend of your father's and an old family friend to us all. He runs the Mesquite Rodeo still and is looking to broaden his holdings out our way." She smiled into his face.

"And my relationships." He turned to everyone at the table. "I'm trying to convince your Mama to date me. Plain and simple. But I'm also here on business. Nash and I have a lot to discuss, and I have some ideas about ways to partner with the Dawson brand."

Mav stiffened immediately, but Nash cut off whatever he might want to say. "After dinner, we should lay it all out for those who want to listen." He squeezed Emery's hand.

"I'd like to hear these proposals myself." Mav's face was blank. With any luck, he wouldn't be too opposed.

"And now I think we should express our thanks before the food gets cold." Mama reached toward Grace, who sat at her other side, and everyone at the table held hands.

"Let us pray." Mama bowed her head. "We thank Thee for this gathering around our table. We've had many a group gather here, and of them all, this feels complete. We thank Thee for the gift of friends, and love. We thank Thee for our bounteous blessings, for all that Father has left for us to care for. And we as always acknowledge him in our lives, knowing he's smiling down from heaven. That he . . ." Her voice wavered. Every eye at the table shot up to her face, which was bowed, her mouth trembling. "That he smiles upon our new relationships. We thank Thee for the love of Thy Son our Savior. Amen."

Mama's eyes were full, her face at peace. The expression she turned to Billy was one of joy and happiness. Nash nodded in approval.

But Mav kicked him under the table.

"Ow, you rat. Those boot tips are sharp," Nash murmured.

"Don't be nodding in support until we know the full story."

"What are you talking about?" Their whispers would soon be noticed by the others certainly.

"What kinds of business deals is he talking about?"

Nash rubbed his shin. "Can we talk about this later?"

Mama was looking from one to the other. "And now let's eat." She smiled.

Everyone grabbed the nearest dish, took some, and passed it on.

Mama's food made everyone feel better. Though at this point in her life, they paid a cook to do most of the work, she still oversaw every detail. Grace helped quite a bit too. That Grace was going to be a mini-Mama before long, and no one would be one bit sad about it.

"Grace. Tell us about all the kids and the pigs." Nash loved to talk about the pigs.

"Well, my biggest and most prized pig is still alive and well."

Mav snorted.

Nash laughed. "Happy to hear my namesake is still so well beloved."

"Don't even get me started." Mav piled the mashed potatoes on his plate.

"But really, the town has showed up to support. Every family has a kid involved, I think. We've got 4-H running like never before and lots of them are entered in the fair this week. We're hoping for a good showing at the Mutton Bustin'. And . . ." She grinned. "We've just got word that it will be televised nationally."

Nash's mouth fell open. "Wait, seriously?" He glanced nervously at Emery.

"Why? You got a problem being the king of the rodeo on national television?"

"Yes, actually, I might."

Billy shook his head. "No, son, this is great. This means your sponsor is happy and the Dawson brand is happy. All you two have to do is smile and pretend you're also happy."

Emery groaned, but then she nodded. "We can do that. We don't have to do anything too embarrassing, right?"

Everyone at the table shared looks back and forth until Emery put her hands down on the table. "What? Someone just say it."

"You're entered in all the sideshow events as well as barrel racing and bull riding." Grace smiled. "Which means you'll be working with me?" She shrugged. "We've added some new things that the younger crowds might like, to modernize the whole event, you know?"

Emery nodded slowly. "So what kinds of modernizing are we talking about?"

Grace looked to Nash for help.

"I don't have any idea what you're talking about Grace. Just spit it out."

"We added a few different things, like mud wrestling for the women?" She winced. "And pie-throwing contests and a dunk tank for the guys." She toyed with her food when Emery and Nash didn't respond right away. "We figured the more publicity you could bring to the event, the better for Willow Creek and the Dawson brand, as well as the other sponsorships, so win-win?" She dared a peek.

Emery grinned. "I'm in! As long as I get to throw a pie at Nash."

"Done." Grace lifted a glass toward her and then they both drank their water.

Nash didn't say much else and the conversation moved on. But how was Emery going to mud wrestle with a broken shoulder?

She shot him a warning glance and he just kept his mouth closed. Really, he didn't mind all the fun. Especially if he was going to be up on a bull. What he didn't want was to be permanently relegated to clown status in the arena. Those guys weren't even the fighters anymore. They were pure entertainment. He'd walk away from rodeo before he became an ornament.

They ate in peace for the rest of the meal. And then right before the dessert would come out, Nash called over to Billy, "Tell us some more about yourself. Your personal self. We know all about your tough-as-nails, rodeo-running self. But you know, what do you like to do?"

He nodded to Nash, then leaned back in his chair. His arms were still as thick as trunks, his neck and chest broad. Even as an older cowboy, the man still had it. "That's a bit of a tough question to answer. I think all of us spend our life just doing the rodeo things. But I love ranching. I love a homestead and the stock. My heart's in the whole business, even in the crops that feed the animals." He drank the rest of his water and someone passed him the pitcher. "But I enjoy a good game of chess." He filled his cup and lifted it to drink again. "And gin rummy. I always win at gin rummy."

"Do you hear that, brothers? That sounded like a challenge," Dylan said as he brought in the cake platter. "First one to beat Billy in gin rummy gets to throw the first pie at Nash."

They laughed and talked, sitting around the big Dawson table until late into the night. The lingering, the fun, the comfortable conversations were things that Nash forgot he was missing. Watching Emery and Lacey drink it all in gave him a whole new appreciation for family, for *his* family. Emery was right. He had it good, to know that no matter what happened, he had the Dawsons. He had his home. They had each other.

He brought her hand to his lips without thinking. He was going to offer all of this to her. He was always pretty proud to be a Dawson, but now, in this moment, his pride was for all new reasons.

Eventually, Mav stood. "I'm on cleanup. And then I say we move into the family room to discuss business."

Everyone groaned.

Nash laughed. "I say we determine who's going to throw the first pie."

They cheered.

"And we all help clean up."

They stood, and within a matter of minutes, with all those hands, dinner was put away and dishes were in the machine.

CHAPTER 19

*E*mery went to bed that night brimming with joy, with Lacey at her side. "Have you ever seen such a happy place?" Emery asked. "They're this utopic situation. This is good for us, for you."

"They aren't perfect, you know." Lacey's tone was a bit more abrasive than she was expecting.

"Of course not. But what do you mean by that?"

"Just that Mav is all up in arms about Billy showing up ready to talk business. Grace is trying really hard to impress everyone by what she does. She could just be Grace and still be loved. Mama is worried about what her sons think when she should grab hold of her life and embrace the new happiness in Billy. The wives seem happy. They're busy in their own stuff. I think you and I could be really happy here with or without the Dawsons and their issues."

"I don't really think any of that would be considered an issue. They're just a normal family with normal stuff to work through."

"But you're all about them being so perfect. And you even

used the work utopic. I just want to point out they're not. No one is. And we've had it pretty good without any of that. You've done great by us, and we've worked hard, and well, I feel like you're knocking yourself because we haven't had the traditional family in our lives. You did good, sis."

Emery smiled and scootched over to pull her sister into her arms. "Thank you, Lace. I worry so much about all that you never had."

"And what about what you never had? We're in this together. Think about what we did, what we do have. We have a house, for crying out loud. Right down the street from these guys. And it's just the two of us. Let that sink in for a minute."

Emery smiled. "You're right. And I do feel grateful, and I recognize our blessings." She needed to bring up Nash and working together with him. She had to do it. Now was the perfect time. But she didn't want to ruin the independent, strong vibes Lacey was feeling. She'd tell her later. Instead, they fell asleep, each contented for their own reasons.

The next day was full of rodeo rehearsals. Emery took the maximum amount of painkillers allowed as soon as she got out of bed, and then pushed through the day.

Luckily, there was nothing to do for the mud wrestling or the other side activities, nothing to rehearse anyway. Those were better played out unrehearsed, Grace told her. The moments where she had the most fun were surprisingly those with Nash at her side, riding in on their horses as rodeo royalty. Their costumes were amazing. And the parade would be full of fanfare and pomp, and she basically planned to enjoy every second of it.

While Emery was all smiles through it all, Nash seemed distracted.

After a few different events where Emery was repeating instructions to him, she waved a hand in his face. "Where are you? Come back. Focus."

He shook his head. "I'm so sorry. I really am not paying much attention, am I?"

"No, you're not. Is everything okay?"

"Yes, better than okay. You're here. That's amazing to me. And you fit right in." He grinned.

"But what?"

"Well, Mav is grumbling. No one knows about our plans. Billy isn't a contributing financial partner or anything. I just think it's going to go down a little tougher than we were hoping."

She considered his words. "Do you think you and Mav should talk about it alone first? To warn him? Might not be great to see his full reaction in front of Billy."

"I've been thinking along those lines myself. I just don't want to have the conversation at all." Nash took off his hat to shake his hair a moment and then replaced it. "Would you come with me?"

A rush of happiness filled her. "Of course. I'd love to be a part."

"He might be more excited about it if you're there, or at least act like he is."

"Then let's do it. Right now." She pointed to Maverick, who was walking across the arena dirt toward the bulls.

"What's he doing over by the bulls?" Nash sat up taller.

"He used to ride, didn't he?"

"Yes, used to. I hope my big brother isn't thinking about getting back up on a bull."

"He holds the record?" She knew she should just stop talking about Maverick and bull riding the minute Nash stiffened. "You're right. His time has passed. Come on, let's talk to him about our ideas."

They rode over to Mav just as he stepped up on one of the chutes. He knew they were behind him without turning. "I miss these days, you know. This chute. The smell. I should have kept riding."

Nash seemed taken aback. But Emery responded. "I understand. It will be difficult to give up."

Mav turned and rested a hand on the side of her horse. "We like to mess around, tease, all that, but you're a blessing here. I want to make sure I tell you that before we all start teasing again. You belong in this imperfect mess of people, and I'm glad you're here."

She felt herself get a little choked up at that. "Thanks, Mav. That means a lot."

"He's just buttering you up so he can win at gin," Nash said.

She laughed. "I don't know if I'm the one to beat. Sounds like Billy has that down."

Mav tipped his hat at his brother. "Nash. Good to see you."

"Mav. We should talk. You got a minute?"

"Sure, right here?"

"Or at lunch. Let's go eat at Marge's."

"You buying? I'm watching, and the prize money you have coming in is no small feat." He whistled. "They didn't have as much to give out when I rode." He looped his thumbs in his jeans and walked with them out of the arena toward their stables.

As soon as they were all sitting around the thick wood tables at Marge's with huge, juicy burgers in front of them, Nash rested a hand on Emery's thigh, which sent her mind in a huge, distracting whirl of memories in the hay. He winked as if he knew. And then he cleared his throat. "We want to join up, Emery and I."

Mav looked from one to the other and then tilted his head. "I . . . know? I thought the hay was a pretty good indication things were going well."

Nash choked. "Oh no. Sorry. I mean in business. She will be our neighbor, and I have this idea that I want to bring her in on. I've worked it up with Billy."

Mav immediately stiffened. "Billy?"

"Well, yeah. I've been practically living with the man this past month. And I ran my stock management idea by him. He loves it. Wants to invest."

Mav's expression was closed. "You let him help you? I offered the same and you turned me down. You won't even talk about it with me."

"Well, I am now. I'm here, I'm talking." Nash waited. And Emery could see that between the two of them, there was some hurt. Mav wanted to be there for Nash, and the youngest Dawson didn't want the help.

Emery rested a hand on Nash's arm. "I reached out to Nash with some ideas because I have to stop riding."

"What?" Mav said.

"My arm is fractured. I'm pretty done. I had just enough to buy the house, but I need some capital to start building up the stock. I thought even cows to buy and sell, but Nash had a better idea."

"We're both after the same thing. And she even has the land. I can't keep riding either."

Mav sat back, his face pained. "You can't ride anymore?"

"I told everyone the doc said one month only, but what he

really said is, one month and then you really should quit if you value your brain."

Mav nodded slowly. "You haven't told anyone?"

"Nope. But Mav, I was on the brink of having everything I ever wanted, of earning it myself. I wanted to do this, to bring something of value to the family. And I'm almost there."

He kept listening.

"So when Billy heard about my plans and offered up a bull and some capitol, I couldn't turn him down."

"Which bull?" Mav's eyes lit.

"The one you're thinking. Wrestler."

His mouth dropped. "He's offering up Wrestler?" Then he whistled. "That's some stock you'll have."

"*We'll* have. I'm part of the Dawson brand. Just expanding to stock management. We each need our own thing or this family will go under. You know that."

Mav looked from one to the other. "So if Billy is offering up the bull and Emery has the land, what's your role in all this?"

"When you say it like that, I feel a little useless here, brother." Nash laughed.

"He's leasing the land, which will pay for much of the inventory. And he's also accumulating the herd and all the animals. Basically, Nash is doing everything," Emery said.

"That's not true. You've been in on this every step of the way," Nash countered.

"And if you two . . ." Mav pointed from one to the other.

"What?" Nash asked.

"Get married . . . or break up?" He winced. "This is none of my busines, but what then?"

Nash obviously hadn't been expecting that question.

But Emery had already thought it through. "We're signing contracts, same as any other business. And in a way, that's one benefit to Billy. The man serves as a buffer between us most often anyway." She laughed.

"A buffer?"

"Yeah, before Em and I started talking nicely to one another, we didn't really get along."

Mav grinned. "Oh, this is too good."

"And so we fully expect not to agree on everything. Billy is a good third partner in that."

"And what do you want from your family?" Mav's hurt was not hidden very well in his eyes.

"Mav, I wasn't trying to cut you out. Can't you see how I want to add something without draining anything? Everyone else has a thing they contribute and I've just been messing around."

"Winning lots of rodeos."

"Yeah." He grinned. "Can I put the whole thing under the Dawson brand?"

"Absolutely."

"And consult from time to time?"

"Even better." Mav's grin grew.

"Speaking of winning, I'm planning to do just that one last time, and I'm gonna beat your world record."

Mav nodded, the pride in his little brother showing on his face. "I hope you do, brother. And I'm proud to be here for your last ride."

Emery smiled at them both. "But no one knows. So don't let that slip out to the sponsor. We've had enough trouble with him."

"I expect he'll know soon enough," Mav said.

Emery bit into her burger and then moaned in happiness.

"This is the best thing I've ever eaten. Besides your Mama's pie."

They joined her and laughed and dipped fries and finished their burgers.

As they were standing to go, Nash put a hand on Mav's shoulder. "Give Billy a chance. Ma is happier than I've seen her in a long time."

"That's the thing that worries me. She's over there making starry eyes. Who's making all the good business decisions around here?"

Nash nodded. "He's a good man. Why don't you sit down and talk to him yourself to hear what his plans are? Maybe he doesn't even want to combine anything with the businesses. He's got a lot already, you know."

"Maybe." Maverick nodded and led them out of Marge's.

They took the truck back to the house, Emery and Nash wedged together, Emery loving that warm expectation that simmered just below the surface whenever she was near him. The brothers made their own way after that, each doing something in Willow Creek that she didn't need to know much about. Emery had business of her own to conduct, and it involved Isaiah.

CHAPTER 20

The morning of a rodeo always filled Emery with hope and expectation. Wins were ahead. Good friends competing. And now family. Could she think of the Dawsons that way? As family? They certainly treated her as such, but from their own mouths, everyone who stayed at the house was family to them.

She and Nash sat atop their horses side by side as they were about to ride in. They had agreed ahead of time to break protocol right from the start and gallop in at a full run. Then they would turn and join the rest of the processional at their slow and stately pace.

The announcer welcomed everyone. "It's Friday night. You're at a Texas rodeo. It doesn't get any better than this!" The crowd cheered, noise filling the air around them. Emery teared up. "Nash. How can we give this up?"

He reached for her hand. "We aren't giving it up! We'll be the lifeblood of this place."

She looked around, at all the animals in the chutes, in the

stalls, under people in the parade, and she knew he was right. She nodded. "Okay, let's do this."

As soon as the announcer called their names, they tore out of the entrance.

She couldn't hear or see anything much after that, just the ground at her feet, the horse beneath her, and Nash at her side. They circled once in a long race around the perimeter, both their horses lifted their front legs in a salute, and then they pranced in place to the spot at the beginning of a slow and stately processional.

Everything came back into focus.

"That was some ride. Welcome to the royalty, Nash Dawson and Emery Banks."

Following the processional, the kids' events began. Grace led them on in her own parade. Nash and Emery stood up on the slats on the back side of a stall so they could see.

Emery enjoyed watching Nash more than Grace. His eyes lit, and the pride in his face brought tears again to Emery's. Then the announcer said, "Grace and Nash Dawson wish to announce the opening of a new center for children. It will be located next to these fairgrounds and will be dedicated to children and their opportunities to learn in the rodeo way, called The Grace Dawson Center for Children. It's a gift, ladies and gentleman. The Dawson tradition continues in our town as Nash generously donates the building for the city's use."

The crowd erupted in a roar of happiness.

Nash looked away, emotion showing on his face.

Emery pulled him into her arms. "You're a good man, Nash Dawson, and I love you." Then she pulled away, sucking in a breath. "Did I just say that?"

He pulled her closer and rocked her in his arms. "You did. Did you mean it?"

She bit her lip and then nodded. "Yes. I do love you, Nash. I have for a long time. Question is, should I have told you?"

His grin started small and grew so large, she had to laugh at his pure happiness. "Yes, you should have told me, 'cause I love you too. I've just been waiting for you to catch up."

"Catch up? I've been loving you way longer. You're the one who needed to do some catching."

He just shook his head, took off his hat, and pressed his lips to hers in a long, slow, demonstration of just how much he loved her.

When he pulled away, she stared at him in wonder. "You do love me."

He kissed her nose. "Don't ever forget it."

When they separated, she to get ready for barrel racing and then mud wrestling and he to prepare to ride a bull for the first time in a month, she could only skip her walking steps. Today was a good day indeed.

$$* * *$$

NASH HURRIED TO THE BULLS. He hadn't let on, but he was worried about Em. She favored her arm without noticing. It looked worse to him. And there was no way she could mud wrestle with it. Riding should be okay, but even that, while holding the reins, she was lopsided.

But his smile grew. She loved him. "Ha ha!" He kicked his feet up. "That's what I'm talking about."

"What are you talking about?" Mav stepped in time with him. "You getting ready to ride a bull again?"

"Oh, yep. And you know, my Em, she loves me." He laughed. "Told me just now."

Mav grinned. "So happy for you, brother. Now, if she'll just stick around long enough to actually marry you, you're good."

Nash dropped his mouth open. "You don't think she'd pull a Bailey, do you?"

Mav just shook his head. "Nope. I think I'm the lucky sap to be the only Dawson to have a woman leave him at the altar." He clapped him on the shoulder. "But things work out. They really do. You gonna propose?"

Nash's heart leapt to triple time. "Uh."

And then Mav leaned his head back to laugh. "All in good time."

They stood together, watching the biggest, baddest bull in the place. "This animal is gonna win me a record," Nash said.

"I hope he does. He's looking a little friendly today." Mav patted him on the rump. "See? No kicking? No angry snorts?"

"You been feeding carrots to my bull?" Nash scowled.

But Mav held up his arms. "I have not. Let me tell you what I learned. This guy is a sneaky devil. He acts calm just like this. All the way until he's out of the gate, and that's when he springs his devil move. A big spin kick within the first two seconds. It's his trademark move."

Nash eyed the bull with new respect. "Well, I'll be. Thanks, Mav."

"Hey, you're welcome. I'm glad I could do something for you."

"There's a lot you've always done, Mav, can't you see? You're always there. Always doing the sacrificing, building. I'm who I am today because of you."

Mav's eye misted and he clapped Nash on the shoulder. "I guess it's time to do a little on your own?"

"Yes! With the Dawson brand, so not too much on my own." He gripped Mav's shoulder in return. "Thanks for letting me call some of these shots."

"You're welcome. I trust you. And I think I might trust Billy. We had a good talk last night."

Nash knew this was huge for his brother. "He's not Dad."

"No way. But remember, Dad respected him. He once said, 'Doing business with Billy Thornton is a treat. The man is honest, and he delivers.'" Mav leaned down, resting the brim of his hat on the wood railing. "Not sure why I remember that, but it's sure helpful now when I'm trying to trust the man to do good by our ma."

"And don't forget, she's no wilting flower. She can take care of herself in some things, I reckon."

"You're right. Of course."

They stood side by side, just smelling the smells, staring at the bull's backside. Then Mav turned to him. "Break the record for me. Blow it out of the water so that no one else can touch it until our sons get there." He gripped Nash's shoulder again with a strength of emotion Nash didn't know he felt.

"You still miss it?"

"I do. You can't ride forever. But I sure wish I could sometimes."

Nash kicked the dirt around with his toes a minute and then he nodded. "Done. I'll do it for you."

Mav pulled him into a tight hug, one Nash hadn't had from his brother since he was little. "Love you, brother. Thank you."

They separated and Nash nodded. "Love you too."

Nash went to change out of his clothes and look over his gear. Mav had other responsibilities too, and he left Nash to his. Emery would be riding before him, and he didn't want to miss any of it. It didn't *have* to be her last ride. People recovered from broken arms, and barrel racers very rarely fell from their horses.

But all the same, he felt like he should be there, so he didn't watch from the stands. He stood on a stall, peeking through to the arena dirt.

The horses were lined up inside. He knew Emery would be the third one out. And he knew it was gonna be a tough win for her. Several other champions had shown up for this, maybe to try and beat her new world record. Or to at least beat the record holder even if none of them reached the time to hold a new one.

He felt jittery and bounced on his feet, rotating his shoulders and arms and neck,

"You nervous?" Isaiah sauntered over, and Nash nearly tripped over his own boots.

He reached out a hand. "Hey, man. Good to see you." They shook like old times. "What are you doing here?"

"Em called me. She wanted to talk about stock management?" He leaned across the stall railing on his forearms, but turned to Nash. "What's that all about?"

Nash kept his face blank. She'd talked to Isaiah? She wanted to bring him in? That was a hard and fast no. They were careful about who became involved with the Dawson brand and they didn't need a sponsor. They had Billy and their own brand to advertise. But he shrugged. "I don't know what she talked to you about. She didn't let me in on that one."

Isaiah's eyes sharpened. "But you do know your plans.

Look, she wanted Bunson to back a new stock management company, to put their name behind animals that are sight unseen. I just need your assurance that this will be winning stock. We don't need the Bunson name on some weak growth-potential shot." He tipped his hat to Nash.

But Nash was unfazed by him. "If it were up to me, we wouldn't be using your name at all." He leaned back against the fence. "I love the sponsor for my riding, but the stock doesn't need a sponsor. In my opinion." He couldn't wait to talk to Emery about this. What had she been thinking?

"Understood. Sounds like you and your partner need to get on the same page. Also sounds like she's making plans. You know Emery is not one to sit around. She's going to barrel this through no matter what it takes. And if you're not on board with something, she'll do it anyway."

Nash shook his head. "I'm really not here to talk about her with you. I'm sure she'll talk to you about it soon. You flew all the way out here."

"I came to see my royal couple."

Nash laughed. "And how did we do?"

"Awesome. We got some great footage."

"Then it won't be a wasted trip."

Isaiah tapped his hat and then stalked off in the other direction.

Now he needed to talk to Emery. She couldn't be creating relationships with people without talking to him first. Could she?

He'd talked with Billy. But that was before he'd worked everything out with Emery. He and Emery didn't even as yet have a business agreement, let alone a contract. He rubbed his forehead. This was much more complicated than he'd originally thought it would be.

The first barrel racer was announced, and she raced out into the arena. Nash was on edge about Emery, everything else forgotten.

Their times were fine. Emery had better times at practice. She was getting ready. He could see Stargazer prancing in place. Then she steadied and they waited, ready to spring.

The buzzer sounded and she raced out onto the arena floor. They went round the first barrel, closer than she'd ever come, went round the second without toppling it, then the third—the barrel wobbled and the crowd went wild. They circled the fourth, and as she was leaning with the turn, her balance was off. Nash saw it. Some in the crowd saw it too, judging from their gasps. As Stargazer completed the rotation with probably the best time Emery had ever had, the horse jerked forward and Emery called out, grabbing her shoulder, her grip gone form the ropes. She slid to the ground.

The horse skidded to a stop.

Nash tore out onto the arena floor, right behind the medics.

Emery's face was white. She clutched her arm, rolling to the side so she could vomit onto the dirt.

"What's the matter?" He fell to the dirt by her head. "I'm here, Em."

"I can't feel my hand. It went numb. And then I fell." She hurled forward. "But my arm and my shoulder, my neck, it kills." She groaned. "Make it stop. Make it stop."

Her whimpers were too much for Nash. "Do something!" he shouted at the medics, who he'd known most of his life.

They nodded. "We are. On three." The gurney was laid out beside Em and they counted. "One, two, three." They lifted her onto the stretcher. Then a team of two lifted both sides. She called out in pain.

"Be careful," Nash said.

"Don't worry, Nash. We got your girl. We'll take good care of her."

He nodded, then ran after them off the arena floor.

"For those interested, Emery's times would have given her a new world record. Can you believe it folks? Beating the old one. Let's lift our hands in prayer to Emery Banks."

Nash tore around the corner, comforted by the many prayers that would be uttered in that huge arena. It went silent. And he offered his own. "Bless our Emery, God. Bless her."

CHAPTER 21

*How appropriate that I would write in my journal about the valley
of death. I will fear no evil. Will I really not fear? When all is
working against me, can I stay strong in my trust and faith that
God has a plan? I hope so.*

*E*mery lay on the table in the exam room at the
rodeo arena. Nash rushed in. "What's going on?
They wouldn't let me in at first."

"Yeah, they were checking my organs and I had to put on
this robe." She looked away.

"Oh, hey now. What is it? How is your arm?"

"Still numb. They aren't sure what's going on. But they
did an X-ray, and ordered an MRI or CT scan or something.
And I don't have the insurance to cover this."

"Don't worry. Your sponsor does." Nash grinned.

She nodded.

"Or your boyfriend. Either way, we got it covered."

"I talked to Isaiah about sponsoring the stock management company."

"He told me."

"Are you mad?"

"I wish you had told me. These are things we talk about. I just want to know why you did it? You still in?"

She nodded. "I don't even want him to. But I panicked. What if we don't get enough money? What if I can't afford the house? What if you and I break up? What if I get kicked out of my new house before I even move in?" She started breathing in a panicky kind of way, and her monitors went off.

The medics rushed back in. One of them frowned in Nash's direction. Emery waved them in. "I'm just stressing. I have too much to worry about right now."

"Then we just focus on the now. What do we need to know now?" Nash asked.

He and Emery both looked at the medics.

"The first thing you can do is calm yourself. Control your breathing. Your racing heart is making our monitors freak out, and that's not a good report for the doctor to see."

"When will the doctor get here?" Nash checked his watch.

"Hey, don't you have bulls?" Emery asked.

His face drained of color but he stayed put. "I'm here if you need me."

"I don't need you." She waved him out. "Go! And win!"

He saluted. "Yes, ma'am." Then he leaned down and kissed her full on the mouth. "I'll see you in eight seconds."

She laughed. "Okay, okay."

Then he ran out the door.

"Tell me." She looked at the medics. "I know the doc is supposed to explain the scans, but is it good or bad?"

Neither medic said anything, but one of them shook his head, just enough.

"I see."

The other medic slugged him in the arm.

"I said nothing. I did nothing. She's making her own conclusions."

Emery tried to cross her arms, but the one was still numb. It felt much like a dried, old fish. "Can someone page Lacey or Mrs. Dawson?" She knew that woman would know what to do. "Or Billy. How about all three?"

They nodded.

When she was once again alone, she considered everything she knew, all her options. She had already planned on retiring. Why did she feel so deflated when the prospect now seemed forced? She laughed to herself. How ironic. The moment she got a sponsor was the very last rodeo she would ever do as a barrel racer.

Unless they could fix her arm.

Because she could still do rodeo. She could teach kids to ride. She could participate in local rides. There was a lot she could do with rodeo without trying to chase down prize money like she had. But all of that would require the use of her arm. Why was it numb? Her thoughts whirled around her in an unrelenting frenzy.

NASH SAT up on the bull in the chute. This devil bull was as calm as the sea. But Mav had warned him, and so he was ready. It would look good for the judges, too, if the bull went crazy straight out of the gate. Especially if Nash hung on.

The chute boss had a hold on the cinch. He was ready to signal the gate. The crowds were listening to the announcer babble on about things. Nash tuned him out. He adjusted his grip. His gloves were worn and comfortable. The ropes were secure. One hand rose into the air. His legs adjusted. Everything went quiet. And then the signal. The gate opened. And sure enough, as soon as the animal was clear of the gate, he went berserk. He jumped, he kicked, he swung his body around in huge contortions. He leapt in great bounds. Nash had never experienced a longer eight seconds. The world continued in slow motion. And all he could do was hang on.

At last, the buzzer sounded. Nash slipped off. And the bull changed personalities again, prancing off toward his stall to the promise of food and water.

"He's psycho," Nash muttered, watching him go. Then he turned for the scores. A perfect lineup so far. His mouth dropped, and he waited. The crowd went silent. The last judge's score lit the screen. A perfect score! The announcer went crazy. The crowd went crazy. Nash stood stock still, with his mouth still open, until his brothers ran into him. Maverick, Dylan, and Decker all hugged him and then lifted him up on their shoulders.

"Nash Dawson just won himself a perfect score. There are only two other riders in the history of bull riding who have ever gotten a perfect score." Nash mumbled their names. "And now our Nash Dawson will be added to theirs. You'll find him in every cowboy hall of fame across the country. Starting with ours here in Willow Creek." The announcer continued, but Nash stopped listening and met Mav's gaze. He nodded, and Nash tipped his hat.

They carried him around the arena one full time on their shoulders and then someone brought him his horse. He climbed up and they raced back around again. The crowd cheered and screamed and stood on their feet. Nash found

Mama and blew her a kiss. She and Billy waved and laughed and carried on. And Nash missed Emery.

He guided his horse toward the exit, squeezed his thighs, and took off and out of the arena. Someone helped him with his horse and Nash kept right on going.

Emery's door was open. The doctor was inside.

But her face did not seem pleased. The doctor was explaining something. Her gaze shifted. She burst into tears when she saw him and held out her hand.

Nash raced to her and wrapped her up in his arms. "What is it? What's wrong, Em?"

He settled on the bed next to her and they both turned their eyes to the doctor.

"Could you repeat all that for Nash. I'm afraid I didn't understand half of it."

"Of course. Emery, you have a pinched nerve and a broken bone in your arm. You will be just fine."

She gasped. "Oh, thank heavens. I thought it was something terrible."

"It has a complicated name. I apologize for not being more clear. And it can look terrible on the scans, but it really is something you should recover from fully."

She nodded. "So when should I get the feeling back?"

"Tonight? Tomorrow? Please call the office if more than two days go by with a numb arm."

"And can I ride again?"

"Absolutely. Once your break heals."

"Yes, sir." She grinned, and then she turned to Nash. "What happened? We heard everyone go crazy."

Lacey rushed in. "Our Nash just got a perfect score."

Emery put a hand at her heart. "No!"

"Yes!" Nash laughed. "I'm amazed. Mav gave me some tips

209

about that particular bull, and he was right, so right. I held on. And wow." He wet his lips. "I still can't really understand it all even though I know. I know, but . . ."

"It means you're one of the greats. You will be talked of for years. At least for all of your life. Your children and their children will mention the fact over dinner," Emery said.

Nash's heart leapt at the thought. "I have some thoughts about these children."

"Oh? Do you?" Her face heated through.

"And this is where I exit." Lacey waved over the back of her shoulder.

One of the medics called after her, "Hey, want to get drinks later?"

Nash turned back to Emery, and he knew he'd found his future. Right here in front of him was everything he'd ever wanted. And all he could do was smile. "So, cowboy," she said.

He ran his finger along her hairline. "I'm so happy you're well."

"Me too."

"They say you would have beat your own record if you'd have been able to finish."

She nodded, and then shrugged with one arm. "I'm okay leaving it all behind. Now that I know I can still compete if I want to, I can do local things. I can work with the kids, whatever I want—that takes all the bitterness away. I'm ready to start working with the animals."

"The first thing I want to do is buy that bull."

She laughed. "Done. We need a great bull. And if he got you your perfect score, everyone's gonna want to ride him."

"And we're gonna want him to have little baby bulls who are just as sneaky."

"Exactly, partner."

"Oh, I like the sound of that. Partner." He kissed her fingers. "But there's something I'd like a whole lot more."

"Oh? And what's that?"

"Husband."

She sucked in a breath.

"Hold that thought." He leaned near, his mouth close to her ear. "I refuse to talk about proposals in the medic's room at the rodeo."

She nodded and then laughed. The monitors all started to beep. "You better think of something super creative. The other Dawson women were telling me about their proposals." She laughed and tugged off the heart sensors.

He laughed too, and then stopped. "Wait, what? Were they really epic or something?" He ran a hand through his hair. "I can't remember a single one."

Emery shrugged. "Who's to say what's epic and what's not?" She tugged him closer. "I think everything you do is epic." Her grin was so delicious he kissed her again.

"And that's a promise for more."

CHAPTER 22

*I*n the week that followed, Nash let Isaiah know they would not need a sponsor for the new company. Then he solidified things with Billy and worked out a contract with the Dawson family. He would be in a joint venture with them. Emery signed the closing documents on her new home. She was healing nicely.

Billy spent more time with the family than away, and everyone was starting to come to expect his presence. One thing they all appreciated was his new interest in cooking.

Grace was doing well in school and helping to design the new building.

Mama seemed happier than ever, and all the wives in the family were expecting babies.

But Nash had still not proposed.

Every time they went out, every time he took Emery for a walk, he knew she was wondering if that was the moment he would ask her.

But he couldn't think of a creative way to show the woman he loved just how much he loved her. He wanted to ask her in a way she would remember forever, that helped her see she was his everything.

Nothing came to mind.

They'd already kissed in the hayfield. Everything seemed a bit anticlimactic after that. He should know—they'd repeated the experience.

But it was time to be engaged. It was time she knew he wanted to spend the rest of his life with her, not just as a business partner but as her husband.

He even googled proposal ideas. But those were someone else's. He didn't want to copy some guy's idea for Emery. The more he thought about it, the fewer ideas he had, until his mind went completely blank.

He woke up early that morning and came down for a drink of milk. Today, he would find a way.

Mama sat at the kitchen table with a mug, in front of their thick family Bible. Something steamy warmed in the pot on the stove.

"What are you drinking?"

"Just some warm milk. It calms my stomach."

"I could use some of that right now."

"Help yourself. I made extra."

"You always know."

She clucked. "I don't think I knew today, though maybe I did." She pointed to a verse. "Will you look at that? It doesn't matter how many times you read the Bible, something new will always leap out at you. This time, it's a doozy."

He laughed. "I gotta see this. Show me the doozy."

With a full mug of warm milk, he joined his mother at the table, looking over her shoulder.

"Here it is, right there."

She pointed, and Nash read, "Do everything in love."

"Yes. Do you see it?"

He tilted his head, considering his mother. "It seems a tall order. Everything?"

"I agree, but consider what a difference that would make on the whole earth if even the most mundane of tasks was completed with love?"

He tapped his fingers against his mug. "Okay, let's test it for a second. What is the worst chore?"

She rubbed her hands together. "Most people would say mucking out the stables."

"Why do you say most people?"

"Because I don't mind it. I feel bad for the animals having to stand in the manure, so I like clearing it out."

"Ah-ha! So you've already proven your point. Your love for the animals. You muck out the stalls with love." He sipped his milk, not at all surprised his mother would feel such a thing. "But what about taking out the garbage?"

"You don't want it in the home, disturbing the peace of those who live there."

"And what about love for the guys who pick up the garbage off the street? Does love for them change the way you actually set the garbage out?"

She starting nodding slowly and then more vigorously. "Yes. Because if you know how they do things, you could set things out to be as easy for them as possible."

Nash nodded. "Yes, I see." He lifted his mug to hers. "This is a doozy."

"So, tell me about your proposal plans for our Emery."

"Why does everyone know I'm thinking about proposing?"

"Because you've told us you are." Mama smiled and patted his arm. "What's holding you back?"

"Oh, nothing at all. I would have been engaged last month if I could just think of a worthy way to ask her. She's expecting something amazing, and I just don't have anything amazing in my brain." He poured himself some more milk, mostly so he had an excuse to keep sitting there talking to Mama.

"So what if we apply this new scripture to your proposal? If you do it with love, how would it look?"

He closed his eyes, picturing Emery's face. "I would hold her close and tell her how much I will love and cherish her. And then I would ask her if she would be my wife."

Mama nodded. "No extras?"

"Nope. That's what love would have me do." He stood. "I got it, Mama! Thank you!"

She waved to him as he ran out of the kitchen, and he heard her laugh as the door closed.

Nash couldn't run fast enough to Emery's home. The ring banged against his chest from his upper pocket. He carried it with him most of the time, hoping for a moment to present itself. But now he knew what that moment would be.

And he had an awesome new focus for them, for him, as he tried to be a good husband. "Do everything in love."

He ran right to her front door and knocked.

And then he realized it was still really early in the morning, like not even seven yet. He backed up slowly, trying not to make any noise on their porch.

But an upper window opened. "Is that you, Nash?" Lacey's voice carried out over the front yard.

"Yeah, but I just realized how early it is. Go back to sleep, I'm sorry."

"I'm awake." Emery's voice came from deeper inside the house. "Come in. There's a key under the mat."

He opened the door and walked in their front area with a sense of deep satisfaction. It was beautiful. The hardwood shone, the chandelier sparkled. The banister and stair railings matched everything just right. They'd spent many hours working on all those details. "Take your time. I'm just gonna get myself some water."

"I'll be right down."

Her soft steps on the stairs made him smile. He listened for her coming around the corner and then watched her enter the kitchen. His mouth went completely dry. She wore her pajamas, which looked to him like the most glorious bit of fabric in the world. Shorty shorts and a silky tank top with a robe over the top. Wow. He smiled. "Good morning, beautiful."

"Good morning." She ran her fingers through his hair. "I like you first thing in the morning."

She was still drowsy and her hair was mussed, and Nash decided this was the perfect moment.

"I was talking to Mama just now."

"Oh?" She shuffled through the cupboards, looking for something. "You want something to eat?"

"Nah, I'm good. Come sit by me a minute."

"Just a second. I need a drink too."

When she had settled in next to him, looking as good as he'd ever seen her, he lifted her hand in his. "We were reading the Bible this morning and started talking all about this great verse. It says to do everything in love."

She nodded, her eyes shining. "I love it when you talk Jesus to me."

"Very funny."

"I'm not even kidding. Listening to you ponder about the words of God is my most favorite thing you do."

217

"Oh, well then perfect, because I was thinking about doing everything with love, and I think it would change how I managed my whole life."

"Me too. Should we talk about how we can do it better?"

He shook his head. "Well, yes. That would be good. But for now, I just want to talk to you for a second. I'd like to do everything I do with you in love. I'd like to show you that love every day of our lives. I'd like to serve and communicate and work and laugh and kiss, all of it in love."

She lifted a hand up to his face. "I like the sound of that."

He nodded. "I think if we always did that, even our fights would be in love."

"And we know how to fight."

"But I kind of wonder if all along, they already were. We were getting to know each other and there for each other."

"Yeah, it was also kind of fun all the time, really. Like a fun way to flirt?"

He laughed. "I had a few things to learn about flirting with a beautiful woman, if that's the case."

She ran a hand up his forearm. "You were great. We're so blessed, aren't we?"

"I really think we are. And I want to be in your life every day, every morning, just like this one, seeing you all mussed up and gorgeous, wanting to pull you into my arms and just loving you, loving you with everything that's in me, loving you so much that I can hardly stand to be away. That's why I came so early. I've been up half the night already waiting for you to wake up. I want to be beside you, with my arm around your middle. I want us. I love you."

Emery's eyes welled with tears. "I love you too. What a beautiful thing to say." She reached for one of his hands.

Nash lifted his pocket flap and she gasped. "Is this?"

He nodded. "I don't have anything you can take a picture of, nothing you can post on social media or make a YouTube out of. What I have is love. And I love you, Emery Banks. I love you with enough love to last our lives. I will work at your side. I will help raise our children. I will cook, clean, organize, ride, whatever it takes around here to make our home a place of love. I will be that for you, if you will please be my wife?" He lowered to his knees and held out the ring.

She burst into tears. "This is the most perfect thing I could ever imagine. I love you too, Nash. I'm yours forever. Let's start our mornings together right now." She leaned across the table and kissed him. "Yes."

His grin couldn't get any wider. He picked her up, spun her around, and then kissed her again. "Can we get married tomorrow? I'm so tired of waiting."

"Yes! I have the preacher on hold for whenever we say."

"Wait, are you kidding me right now? Is there anyone we should invite from your side?"

"Just Billy?" She laughed. "And he's probably already here."

"Yep, saw him yesterday. Then we're set. I'm totally and completely serious about getting married tomorrow."

Lacey peeked her head around the corner. "I'm sorry to interrupt, but . . . you can't get married tomorrow. Mama alone would put a stop to it." Then she pulled her head back.

Nash and Emery laughed, and he pulled her close again in the best hug of his life. She fit in all the right ways, and at last, he felt whole. With his chin on the top of her head, he imagined the rest of his mornings with her just like this. "I have a feeling we're going to be very happy."

Her sleepy nod in his arms confirmed it.

EPILOGUE

*E*pilogue

Nash and Emery stood together at the fence, both of them eyes wide. Their bull, the devil bull they called him, was about to sire a new son. They hoped. But a daughter would be a good breeder. Emery gripped the fence. Nash stood close behind her.

Voices alerted them of the others' arrival. Mav, Deck, Dylan, Mama, Billy all arrived one after the other.

Emery laughed. Billy and Mama were holding hands. They were so often together and he was such a part of the family she wasn't surprised at all that a wedding had been mentioned. After she and Nash had married, they were the next focus, them and Grace. Emery grinned. She was totally crushing on a guy her senior year and none of the brothers could handle it, most particularly not Nash, but Emery thought he was a good guy, a true cowboy and that was enough for her.

Grace entered and to Emery's surprise, brought Wyatt with her, their hands tightly intertwined.

They rushed to the fence.

"Welcome to this Dawson family gathering." Nash laughed.

"It's an important occasion. The first home grown stock for our new Stock management arm." Mav held out his fist to bump with Nash.

The animal moaned.

"What's wrong? Is she alright?" Nash called over to the vet who was down on her knees, massaging the animals stomach.

"She's just fine. Probably feeling some discomfort."

Bailey laughed. "Discomfort?" She shook her head. "That animal is in the most pain she's ever felt."

Emery rubbed her stomach. And then Nash's hand joined hers. He kissed the back of her neck. "You're gonna do great."

She smiled and turned to him. "Should we tell them?"

The animal grunted and then someone shouted. "I see it!"

The newest young one was being born.

"Not yet." Nash nuzzled her. And then they both glued their eyes to the birth.

"It's gonna be a bull." The vet called. The animal leapt up. "And a lively one from the looks of him." She laughed.

"I would expect nothing less." Emery turned to Nash. He pulled her closer. "Congratulations." He kissed her softly.

"There was a time I wasn't sure I'd even make it this long." She shook her head, the wonder of her life flowing over her yet again. "Dreams. Here's another one coming true right in front of my eyes."

Nash couldn't smile any larger. But he pulled her close again and just held her because all his dreams were coming true right along with hers.

The End.

READ ALL BOOKS BY SOPHIA SUMMERS

JOIN HERE for all new release announcements, giveaways and the insider scoop of books on sale.

Cowboy Inspired Series
Coming Home to Maverick
Resisting Dylan
Loving Decker
Falling for Nash

Her Billionaire Royals Series:
The Heir
The Crown
The Duke
The Duke's Brother
The Prince
The American
The Spy
The Princess

Read all the books in The Swoony Sports Romances
Hitching the Pitcher
Falling for Centerfield
Charming the Shortstop
Snatching the Catcher
Flirting with First
Kissing on Third

Vacation Billionaires
Holiday Romance

Her Billionaire Cowboys Series:
Her Billionaire Cowboy
Her Billionaire Protector
Her Billionaire in Hiding
Her Billionaire Christmas Secret
Her Billionaire to Remember

Her Love and Marriage Brides Series
The Bride's Secret
The Bride's Cowboy
The Bride's Billionaire

COMING HOME TO MAVERICK
CHAPTER ONE

*M*averick dipped his hat lower against the hot Texas sun. A man's hat could hide a lot of things, unfortunately not everything. His forearms flexed against the rough wood of the split-rail fence, as he stretched his fingers open and closed. His mind was so far away he hardly noticed Colton or the new horse in the small corral used for training horses. This new colt was fighting every effort to break him, and Maverick didn't blame him one bit. He knew his thoughts were ridiculous, but he suddenly wanted that horse on the run, leaping over the fence and taking off across the pasture. Their new trainer was having a devil of a time with the Spawn of Satan, and Maverick wanted to see who would break first—Colton, the trainer, or Spawn, his horse. His bets were on Colton. The horse had passion, fire, and a strong will, exactly what Maverick needed in himself right now.

The tension in the horse's flank, his flared nostrils, and the dance of trainer and horse were familiar, comforting. Maverick imagined himself out there, facing the whip, as he tried to distract himself from the shattering news of a just a few hours ago.

Their property, which stretched for miles in every direction, had always felt like a safe haven. He'd felt God in those hills countless times. But even the stark beauty of the rugged, rocky terrain and rolling green hills couldn't protect him from the news that had sent him out riding the fence line, checking their bales of hay, inspecting the tractors in the back barn, and then finally here to the horse paddock. He'd tried to send some prayers up to Heaven on the way, but at least that afternoon, God was being strangely silent.

His phone rang. "Yeah."

"Where are you?" Dylan's gruff voice made him smile.

"You worried about me?"

"I'm more worried about the paperwork I gotta send to the accountant."

Maverick didn't believe that for a second. "Colton needed some support."

The quiet on the line said more than any response could have. Maverick was hiding. They all knew it.

Maverick grunted. "And I needed some space."

"So you heard."

"How could I not hear when no one can stop talking about it?"

"You coming in for lunch?"

The whole family gathered for lunch every day. It was more like a late breakfast, but it was a family rule that they show up. And for the first time in a long time, Maverick wished he could avoid them, at least for a little while longer. The last time had been when they'd laid their father to rest in the family plot on the northwest corner of their property. His father had been his hero; he'd raised four boys into men, created a successful thriving ranch, and left the Dawson Ranch legacy to Maverick.

And now Maverick's fiancée had returned after six years, with no explanation, no effort to reach out. She just showed back up in their hometown. And he found himself needing some solitude.

Spawn kicked up his back legs and leapt around the paddock, trying to rid himself of the newly placed saddle. Maverick envied the horse. When would it ever be acceptable for Maverick to kick up his heels and buck off whatever he didn't want to deal with?

But he knew he'd best be heading back to the kitchen, or he'd suffer the wrath of Mama. And no one with any sense or brains messed with his mama. He grinned. They owed everything to the strength of that very short woman. "I'll be there."

He heard a grunt of approval or relief or something—who knew what Dylan's grunts meant—and then he hung up the phone. His gaze traveled over the surrounding hills, the patchwork green and tan of the hay they put out every year to feed the livestock. In a couple months, they'd be bringing in the cows to sell at auction. They'd harvest their crops and nestle in for the winter months. The guys would start in on the rodeo circuit, Mama would participate in the local craft shows and fairs, and he'd take a break.

He hopped on the ATV, waved good luck to Colton, who was being controlled by the young horse, and then took the longest path back to the house.

He offered a prayer as he crested the ridge overlooking his family's homestead. "Thank you Lord for all the goodness in our lives, for my brothers and my Mother." He paused, expecting a rush of satisfaction. They'd built something special. The Dawson brothers were known for their cattle, their horses, and their rodeo championships. His father would be proud. They were all fine, honorable men. And according to Dad, that's what mattered. "I don't care what career you choose," he used to say, "but be honest, hardworking, and competent at whatever it is."

Except in Maverick's case, Dad did care what he became. Maverick was the new head of the Dawson Ranch, the new head of the family, as prescribed in the will his father left. Only, Maverick felt like half the man his father had been. He turned the ATV back down the path. His other brothers were pulling up to the house. Time for lunch. He finished his prayer. "I should be grateful, and I am. Help me to show it today even though I've had some hard news." He grit his teeth, knowing he should say the next words, but finding it difficult. "And please bless Bailey. She must have gone through an awful lot. Amen."

A loud, musical horn echoed across the valley, and he shook his head. Nash. Sounded like his youngest brother was in high form. His Jeep spun out in the gravel at the start of the long drive, and then he slowed to a crawl as he approached the house. Maverick nodded to himself. Nash knew better than to throw dust all over Mama's flowers. Mama was continually reminding them that someday they'd have grandkids running around the front yard and they'd all have to be careful.

Grandkids. Maverick had stopped counting how old his kids would have been if he and Bailey had actually been married. They could have had two by then. Or maybe they would have had a long honeymoon relationship with no children. He'd have liked that just as well.

"Stop," he told himself again. Bailey's return to Willow Creek had brought back emotions he thought he'd buried years ago. But pieces of his heart still longed for her and felt as raw as the day she left. Before he could shut out the memory, the view of the long aisle at the church filled his mind—the pews decorated with ribbons and flowers, the floor sprinkled with flower petals. Everyone they knew and loved smiling up at him, his mother's eyes full of tears, and his father's full of pride. He swallowed the lump in his throat before it could turn into anything that would make his eyes red when he walked into lunch with his family.

He drove down the side of the hill and parked his ATV in the garage, wiping off the trail dust and placing the keys on the hook. Then he went through the workroom, tidying the few items out of place. He brushed the dust off himself again, wiped his face, and ran a hand through his hair. His hat went on a hook—no hats at the dinner table. He was about to open the door into the house when his mama's voice stopped him.

"We love you, son. We'll support you in whatever you want to do."

He turned to face her. Her hair was still damp from her shower, the soft curls framing her face. She stood near the entry into the house, watching him, seeing through his stoic front. Mama was a dear, but she had no notion of the private emotions of a man's heart.

"What I want to do?"

Her eyes were kind with a hint of sorrow, and he hated that he was the cause. She handed him some napkins to bring in from the storage room and a bin for extra dishes.

He'd endlessly analyzed the events of his wedding day and he and Bailey's relationship, and still he couldn't imagine how he could have acted differently. And he didn't know what more he could do now. You can't prepare to be blindsided. And he knew his mama had been hurt in her own way.

She'd given her heart to Bailey and had, in some ways, lost a daughter when the woman had left.

Mama nodded. "Yes. We're with you whatever you decide to do—or not do."

He wrapped an arm around her. "I don't know what I want to do. But I do know I love you, Mama. Let's go have some of Cook's food."

She laughed. "The best thing you ever did was hire a cooking staff."

"I see no reason why you have to be the one to make your signature hotcakes."

"Sometimes I go make sure they've got it right," she said with a smile.

"I have no doubt. And they're delicious every time."

She stood on tiptoe. He dipped his head so she could kiss his cheek and give it a pat. "You're a good man, Maverick. You deserve to be happy."

"I am, Mama. What more could a dusty cowpoke need?"

She wiped her hands on the front of her apron and then took it off. She placed it on a hook, and together they entered the house and made their way into the large dining room. Maverick stood in the doorway. All three of his brothers were in town, and each of them sat at the table. Heaping piles of pancakes waited on platters down the center of the table. Almost as much bacon, eggs, toast, and thick slices of ham made his stomach grumble. Instantly, his mood lifted.

"Brothers." He nodded. No one heard him.

Nash stood from his chair. "You can't even go there. If I'm riding Spice, no one's gonna beat me. Not you, not Tommy, no one."

"You're a mess, Nash."

"Take a look in the mirror before you go making comments, Decker. When's the last time you brought home a first place?"

Mama cleared her throat and nodded toward the sign on the wall behind her. "Dawson happiness starts at home."

The brothers grumbled but closed their mouths.

Mama treated this room as the center of their family. She kept their portraits in there, their senior pictures from high school. The wall also held two phrases the family lived by. "If you're unhappy, get to work" was displayed in large sweeping letters on the opposite wall from the one Mama had just quoted. The brothers stood when Mama entered. She sat at the head of the huge, thick wood table that dominated the room. Then her eyes turned to Maverick, alerting his brothers to his presence.

"Hey, Maverick! How's the colt?" Dylan asked. He was the one who took care of the horses, including their training and breeding.

Maverick felt their eyes on him as he moved to sit at the other end of the table. "He lives up to his name. Good test run for Colton, though you're gonna have to save him. Maybe sooner than later."

Dylan nodded. "He'll come around. They both will. Colton came highly recommended. He has a way with horses like no one I've ever seen."

Maverick was grateful they were talking business. "Nash, I heard your new horn."

"Isn't it awesome!" he said, his grin wide. "I'm taking the Jeep with me when the circuit starts."

"You're going this year?" Mama poured herself some water.

Everyone looked at their mother as Nash nodded. "Of

course, I'm going. You said if I finished out two years helping on the ranch, I could spend the next doing the rodeo circuit."

Mama didn't answer. And she avoided Maverick's gaze. If no one else stayed, Maverick was the one who stayed. And so far, he'd been happy with that. He didn't have a problem with taking over for his father; he'd always known some day he would; he'd just thought it would be later. There's nothing else he would rather be doing anyway, he told himself.

Decker, Dylan's twin, usually disagreed with everything Nash said on principle. But he sat quietly, which Maverick found suspicious.

"What are the predictions on the team this year?"

Mama held up a hand. "Wait. Before we get into all that, let's pray."

Everyone waited for Mama to say a few words. "You know I'm proud of you boys. We miss those not with us, your father most of all, but I know he'd be even more proud of every one of you. Thank you for what you give to the ranch. It's a huge endeavor. Your father gave everything he had to this ranch, knowing it would help take care of each of us for as long as we took care of it." Her eyes traveled to each man at the table, and Maverick knew she desperately needed the ranch. He supposed he did too. It was the only thing they had left of their father. If the ranch lived, their father did too. Mama closed her eyes. They held hands around the table and bowed heads.

"Dear Lord bless this family. Bless this land. Bless the women my boys are going to one day marry. And today especially bless Maverick. We're grateful for every thing in our lives that you placed there in such a perfect way, the hard times and the easy. Amen."

They all echoed, "Amen."

Nash raised his fork. "Let's eat!"

Mama nodded. "Let's eat."

Everyone dug in. Maverick slapped away Decker's hand as he reached for the same slice of ham. "Wait your turn."

Nash passed him a dripping, sticky syrup pitcher.

"Hey now, whoa. Go wipe that off," Maverick said.

"Why me?"

Decker snorted. "'Cause you're the one who drizzled syrup all over the handle."

Nash frowned but got up from the table to wipe the sticky drips of syrup off the handle. The Dawsons had no patience for anything sticky.

They'd almost finished the meal when Decker put down his napkin and looked directly at Maverick. "So, what are you gonna do about Bailey?"

Everyone went silent, and the air thickened with expectation. His mother avoided his eyes, but all three pairs of his brother's eyes waited for his response.

"I don't know that there is anything to do."

"What if she comes walking back in, thinking there's still a chance over here?" Decker's eyes flashed with anger.

"I don't think there's any chance of that. She hasn't said a word to me."

Everyone seemed to be waiting for him to say something else about it. So finally, he sat back in his chair. "I don't know, all right. I had no idea she was coming. I don't know why she left. I don't know what she's been doing except what everyone else knows." He'd stopped checking social media years ago. "So I don't know what to tell you. Will I see her again? I imagine I'll run into her the next time I have to go into town." He tried to keep the pain off his face, but it was just too hard to hide. "I'm not gonna pretend I'm okay with it, but I don't know what else to do except move forward as though we are people that barely know one another."

"We could shun her." Nash twirled his fork. "You know, like outright avoid her, refuse to talk to her. If you asked the town, they'd support you. She hurt them when she left, too." He replaced his fork. "Not as much as you, but they might not want to take her back in with open arms, especially if we say we aren't ready."

Maverick held up his hands. "I don't want us to say or do anything. If we see her, we're polite. If we don't, that's fine too." A part of him wanted to see her right away and get it over with. But the other part wanted to go on a long vacation and hope she left before he came back.

COMING HOME TO MAVERICK
CHAPTER TWO

*B*ailey stood as tall as she could, but she knew there was no amount of pretending that could help make coming home any easier. She knew word of her arrival had spread through town as soon as her car drove down Center Street.

She hadn't had time or money to change out her obnoxious license plate, *CTRYSTR*. Who put Country Star on their license plate? Bailey had when she left. She shook her head. She hardly knew that woman anymore. But she hardly knew the woman who'd been raised in this town, either. Just the thought of attending church with the members of her town filled her with shame. So why was she back?

She circled around to the other side of the car and opened the door.

"Are we here, Mama?" Gracie Faith's sweet voice warmed her and, at the same time, filled her with anxiety. She reached for her hand. "Come on, sweet pea. Let's go meet your grandma."

And bless her heart, the girl skipped and squealed. Her face alone could have lit the neighborhood.

Oh, please. Please make this easy. It wasn't quite a prayer. She hadn't prayed in a long time. But she sent her plea to the universe anyway. Maybe God still heard people who were afraid to ask Him for things.

They walked up the sidewalk. Everything was the same. The front porch looked like it had a recent paint job. She counted cracks in the old cement, like always. Then she heard a small voice. "One. Two. Three."

She smiled. Willow Creek was the perfect place to grow up. If she could give her daughter even a portion of what Bailey had when she was younger, she'd give her a good place to grow up at last.

Her stomach clenched. Nothing could erase the first five years of her baby girl's life. They were on the road if Bailey was lucky enough to get a gig, and they ate whatever food Bailey could scrape up. How many times had she watched Gracie sleep on a bench at the local bar while Bailey sang on stage?

The door to her parents' farmhouse opened before they made it halfway up the walk. Bailey's mother clutched at her heart, and her face squinched in joy.

"Bailey!" She ran down the stairs and flung her arms around Bailey. Her bony arms held her desperately. She was considerably skinnier since Bailey had seen her last, and the lines in her face were more visible. But she smelled the same. And as Bailey breathed in her mother, everything in her life shifted one degree closer to where things needed to be.

As soon as her mom let her go, Bailey placed a hand on her daughter's head. "And this is Gracie Faith."

Tears welled up in her mother's eyes, and she knelt carefully in front of Gracie Faith. Her loving mother eyes, the same eyes that had so carefully watched over Bailey as a child, searched Gracie Faith's face. "Are you my granddaughter, darling?"

Gracie nodded. "I think so." She reached out and placed a hand on her mama's face. "You look like my mama."

"She's my baby, just like you're her baby."

Gracie nodded. "Then I'm your granddaughter." She said it so matter-of-factly, Bailey wanted to laugh and sob at the intensity of the moment. She'd dreamed how it would be to introduce Gracie to her family since the day her daughter was born.

"I'm so happy to meet you." Bailey's mom smiled. "Do you wanna come inside? I've got cookies, and I can show you your mama's old room. And then we can do whatever you want. I hope you settle right on in and stay awhile." Her gaze flicked to Bailey, and the hopeful love there nearly broke her heart.

"We've come home, Mama. If you've got room, we'd love to stay awhile." She'd called to tell her mother she was coming and that she had a daughter, but nothing could have prepared either of them for this moment.

Her mother's eyes welled up again, and she just nodded.

Her dad stood in the doorway.

Her mom stopped. "Look, honey. Bailey's come home."

He stared for a moment. His age had not diminished his broad stature one inch. And then his face broke into a huge smile. "Come here, you." He stretched out his arms and pulled Bailey into the safest place she'd ever known. She broke down and allowed all the tears to fall that she'd been holding in since she arrived in Willow Creek. Tears that she'd been holding in since she'd left in the first place, since she'd found out she was pregnant with this precious new soul. As she quietly shook, hoping not to worry her daughter, her father just hugged her, his hand patting her back.

"Is that Grandpa?" Her daughter sounded concerned, so Bailey backed away, wiping her eyes, and said, "Sweet pea, this right here is the greatest man you'll ever meet. Your grandpa loves you, hon."

She stepped forward and tipped her chin up so she could see his face. "Are you a giant?"

His laugh started deep inside and then bubbled over. "No, I'm no giant, but I sure would like to get to know you."

"I'm Gracie Faith."

"Well, come on in, little nugget. Once we get you settled, I'll take you out to the barn to meet all the other guys we got around here." He stopped. "Let's get you unloaded first." They made their way back to the car, and Bailey bit back her embarrassment. The car gave off an obvious homeless vibe.

"Do you like my bed?" Gracie pointed to her pillow in the back seat. "And Mama sleeps up there when she's not driving."

Her dad choked, his eyes getting misty. It was one of the few times she'd ever seen him get emotional.

"That's nice, Gracie. I love the flowers on your pillowcase."

Gracie grinned as she showed off where they'd been living for the last few months, and Bailey just took it, like she'd known she'd have to. The part of her life she'd hoped to never share with her parents was being put on display. She just kept reminding herself that Gracie was worth it. She deserved a house, a bed, and people who loved her.

Her dad hefted a box onto his shoulder and pulled their

one piece of luggage into the house. "Gracie, I can't wait to show you the guys."

"There are more people?"

"He's talking about the horses, love." Mom smiled. "She's gonna go see her room first, dear. And then you can whisk her off to your horses."

"I love horses!" She squealed, and Bailey knew she'd made the right choice in coming home. No matter what it took, she was determined to give her daughter the life she deserved.

When they walked into Bailey's old room, she about doubled over as her stomach clenched in pain. Pictures of her and Maverick were everywhere. The morning she'd spent getting ready for her wedding flashed before her eyes. Nothing in the room had changed. Her hairbrush was right where she'd left it. Her makeup case. The perfume she'd worn that day. She leaned against the doorframe, hoping no one else noticed how shaken she felt. She watched her daughter run around the room, picking up old rodeo trophies, hugging stuffed animals. And then when Gracie climbed up into the large four-poster, Bailey let the tears fall. Her attention drifted to the window overlooking the back pasture. She'd always stood at that window to watch the horses.

"Chester?" Her voice caught in her throat.

"Daddy couldn't sell her. She's out there whenever you're ready."

Her body literally itched to go take a ride, but she had to get Gracie settled first. Tonight, after everyone was in bed, she'd go talk to her horse.

Once they were all settled and Grandpa was showing Gracie how to brush down the horses, Bailey sat with her mom on the porch that overlooked the back paddock and pasture. "You and Dad look great."

"We're blessed with good health. But he's slowing down, only working horses for our friends now. I'm happy at the county fair now and then. Otherwise, we lead a quiet life."

Her mother didn't ask where she'd been. She had to have a million questions, but she didn't ask a single one. She just waited.

"I'm happy to be home. Do you mind if I...stay awhile?"

Her mom's hand reached for hers and squeezed. "You can stay as long as you like. You and your daughter are always welcome."

"Thanks, Mom." Her throat felt tight again. They had a lifetime, she hoped, to talk about what had happened, about why she hadn't been able to face them with her poor choices. How did one own up to leaving her fiancé at the altar? And then living with another man, having his baby, getting thrown out with nowhere to go, and utterly failing in every area of her life? She didn't know. And so she never had. It had taken every bit of grit she had left to come home. And now that she'd returned, it was enough to just sit at her mom's side.

As she exhaled slowly and let the remaining tension leave her body, she thought about the last time she'd sat on this porch.

With Maverick.

His strong hand had covered both of hers. "I'm always here for you. That's what forever is all about."

She hadn't believed him. She felt sure that if she told him she wanted to explore her music before getting married, that she was suffocating in their small town, yearning for space, for freedom, that he would give up on her. Everyone wanted to marry Maverick Dawson. The Dawson brothers were where life started and stopped in this town.

Another sigh escaped before she could stifle it.

"He's still single, you know."

"I know." She wasn't even surprised her mama knew what she was thinking. But she didn't want to think about Maverick. Not yet.

Dad and Gracie walked toward them, hand in hand.

"She's such a beautiful child, and she has a good heart. You can see it in her eyes."

"She really is, Mama. She's something special. I just want to give her what I had."

"I'm so happy to be in her life. I didn't even know..." She reached for Bailey's hand again. "Sorry. You had your reasons, and I trust that."

Bailey just nodded. "I'll talk about it when I can. I—I'm sorry." Her voice broke, and she looked away.

"No, no, honey. I'm just here to love on you. That's all that's needed right now."

Gracie bounded up the stairs and threw her arms around Bailey. "Mama! You should see the horses! Grandpa said he'd teach me to ride! He has the prettiest pony. Can I, Mama? Please?"

Bailey's eyes welled with tears again. "Of course, darling. That's why we're home."

Long after Gracie was in bed, Bailey sat on a couch in the living room, curled up with a blanket, a book in her lap. "I miss Red." Her golden retriever had never left her side when she was home. She loved that dog. He had known all her secrets and took them to his grave while she was gone.

Her dad sat up. "Gracie Faith needs a dog."

Her mom was about to shake her head, but Dad held up a finger. "No child can grow up without a dog to love her."

"You guys don't have to get a dog," Bailey said.

"Of course, we do. I'll take her to the shelter tomorrow. If there's not a good one for kids, we'll look around for puppy announcements. Someone's always trying to get rid of some of their litter around here."

Bailey didn't have the heart to argue. Her parents loved to help and wanted nothing more than to do nice things for her and her daughter. She'd been blessed well beyond what she deserved. "I don't think she's gonna know what to do with herself. First grandparents, then horses, and now a pet dog." She pulled the blanket up tighter around her even though she wasn't cold. "Thank you."

Her dad chuckled. "Well now, there's no thanking us."

"Yes, honey. We love you. You know that." Her mother's words were comforting, but her eyes held a hint of insecurity that Bailey wished she'd never put there.

"I need to tell you guys why I left."

Dad held up his hand. "When you're ready. We trust you."

"Thank you. I'm not even sure I know, really. I was…I was thinking about marriage to Maverick, about living here my whole life, about all my dreams of singing and going to Nashville—you know how when I was a little girl I used to go out back and sing to the orchard?"

"That's where it all started." Her mom smiled. "And then at church and in the county fair."

"Well, over time I realized that wasn't enough, but I never told anybody. I figured I had a good life, a good man, a good future. I should be happy. But I'd never been anywhere. College was only an hour away, and Maverick was my only boyfriend." She closed her eyes and leaned her head back.

"Nobody knew you weren't happy."

"I don't even know if *I* knew I was unhappy. That's the thing. I didn't know myself at all. And I got scared and took off for Nashville. What I did was so terrible that I didn't dare contact you, and then it became easier not to—and then it became too long of a time I'd let slip by." She forced herself to meet their eyes. "I was living a life I now you don't approve of. And then Gracie…"

"Sounds like you're well on your way to figuring things out," her dad said.

Bailey smiled ruefully. "Hopefully I can figure it out before I have to talk to Maverick."

"Everybody makes mistakes. It's been five years. He's a good man."

"You'll feel better when you do," her mom urged.

"I know I was unhappy, and I needed to communicate better, but what I lacked most of all was gratitude and courage. And for that, I'm so sorry. I'm sorry I left without telling you and that I didn't talk to you all these years." She swallowed. "I know that's not good enough, just saying sorry when you do something that big, that hurtful. It's gonna take some time for you to forgive me. But I'll make it up to you, pay you back, work the ranch. I'll prove again that I can be the daughter you deserve."

"Oh, honey, no." Her mom jumped up and sat as close as she could to Bailey. "That's not how it works with us. And that's not how it works with God either. You keep talking to Him. He'll let you know. And as far as your Daddy and me, we forgave you years ago."

"Oh, I don't talk to Him any more. How can I when I let everyone down like I did? Maverick…." She shook her head.

"I just don't think God wants to hear much from me anymore."

"Well, it's times like this when you need to talk to Him the most. He's way better than your Daddy or I am about forgiving." She patted her knee. "Honey, there is nothing ever that can separate you from the love of our Lord."

"That's the absolute truth. You can read that in Romans eight if you want to remember." Her dad shook his head. "Don't you worry about us. Just like your Mother said, we've already forgiven you. Long time ago."

She nodded, but she didn't know what to say. She would do whatever she could to help these parents of hers who deserved so much. But she didn't think she could ever make it right with Jesus, not after all she'd done. "I wish I had come back years ago."

"Looked like you were kind of busy."

"Singing in some local places."

Bailey started. "What? Did you come?"

"Did we come? Your mother made a book."

"She did?" Bailey was shocked when Mom brought out a thick three-ring binder packed with pages and handed it to her. Her lap felt weighed down with the pages.

"We started this as a wedding gift."

The first page was a double spread of her and Maverick as kids—their elementary school pictures and others. She skipped ahead, grazing past the pre-wedding shots, the bridals, the engagements. And then she stopped at a pair of tickets to her first gig and a picture of her parents standing together in front of the venue.

"You were there?" She couldn't stop the tears. They were too kind. "You were there?" Had they tried to come see her backstage? Had security bounced them out? Had they just watched and left? She couldn't handle the answers to those questions, so she set the binder aside. "I'm sorry. I didn't even know." She stood, not even able to stand her own self. "I think I need time to let this settle. Can I look at it later?"

"Of course." Mom shut the book as Bailey hurried from the room, choking back sobs.

When she was back in the guest room, she dried her tears and lay back in her bed. As she tried to drift off to sleep, Maverick's face came into her mind. She'd grown up with him. They had memories from every year of her life until she'd left. But the face she saw now was not the childhood Maverick but the man who'd loved her. The man who had cupped her cheeks in his large, rough hands and kissed her softly, tenderly, over and over until she didn't know what to do with the yearning that swelled up inside. That's the Maverick that lulled her to sleep as she hugged a pillow and wished she didn't have to tell him what she'd done.